A cupboard full of coats

YVVETTE EDWARDS

ONEWORLD
OXFORD

A Oneworld Book

Published by Oneworld Publications 2011

ISBN 978-1-85168-797-8 (Trade paperback)
ISBN 978-1-85168-836-4 (Travel edition)

Typeset by Glyph International
Cover design by Ghost
Printed and bound in Great Britain by CPI Mackays

Oneworld Publications
185 Banbury Road
Oxford OX2 7AR
England

Learn more about Oneworld. Join our mailing list to
find our about our latest titles and special offers at:
www.oneworld-publications.com

A Cupboard Full of Coats

1

It was early spring when Lemon arrived, while the crocuses in the front garden were flowering and before the daffodil buds had opened, the Friday evening of a long, slow February, and I had expected when I opened the front door to find an energy salesperson standing there, or a charity worker selling badges, or any one of a thousand random insignificant people whose existence meant nothing to me or my world.

He just knocked, that was all, knocked the front door and waited, like he'd just come back with the paper from the corner shop, and the fourteen years since he'd last stood there, the fourteen years since the night I'd killed my mother, hadn't really happened at all.

I had imagined that moment a thousand times; Lemon had come back for me. He knew everything yet still loved me. Over a decade filled with dreams where he did nothing but hold me close while I cried. Had he come sooner, my whole life might have panned out differently and it might have been possible to smile without effort, or been able to love. Had he come back before, I might have been happier in the realm of the living than that of the dead, but he had left it too late and things were so set now I could hardly see the point of him coming at all. Yet there he was.

He stood there in the cold, wet and wordless. He offered no excuses or explanations; no *I was just passing through and thought I might stop by*. He didn't tip a cap or smile and enquire after my health, nothing. He stood there watching me as if he wasn't sure whether I might throw my arms around his neck with a welcoming shriek or slam the front door in his face. But I did neither. Instead I watched him back, till eventually he gave a small shrug that could have meant just about anything.

He had what my mother had always called 'high colour', a black man with the skin of a tanned English gentleman, and like a gentleman, he had always dressed neatly. In that respect, he hadn't changed at all.

His taste in clothes seemed the same a decade and a half later, or maybe he'd just found himself stuck with the wardrobe he'd purchased in his youth. He wore Farah slacks that day and a Gabicci suede-trimmed cardigan with a Crombie overcoat thrown casually over them.

Though the rain had stopped, he was thoroughly soaked through, from his hair – which he had always kept skiffled low but which was longer now: a silver-tinged Afro that was damp and forged into steaming tufts – to the lizard-skin shoes on his feet. But though his clothes were still the same, *he* had aged. There were changes around his face; the crow's feet at the corner of his eyes were wider fanned, the bags beneath them full and heavy, and his old skin bore new lines. His eyes were red-rimmed, the whites yellowed, the expression intense as he looked at me, already asking questions, talking of things that should be whispered even when alone, and it was me that looked away, looked down, wondering if my own eyes were as eloquent as his, afraid that they might be speaking volumes, scared of the things they might have already said.

I opened the front door wide as he wiped his feet on the mat outside. It used to say Welcome, but was so faded now, only someone who knew what it had said before would be able to guess the word had ever been there at all. He bounded over the step like a cat, lithe-footed. He had always been a good mover, the kind of man you could not take your eyes off when he danced, the kind of man you had to drag your eyes off, period. I closed the front door quietly behind him.

He was in.

He stood inside the hallway looking around. I had done a lot with the house in the time he'd been away. The green doors and skirtings had been stripped. The old foam-backed carpet had been replaced with laminated flooring. The last time he'd been here, the walls were covered in deep plum velvet-embossed wallpaper; now they were smooth, clean, white. I sniffed.

'You need a bath,' I said.

He nodded. I walked up the stairs to the bathroom and he followed. I turned on the taps and the tub began to fill.

'I'll get you a towel.'

I left him in the bathroom while I went in search of a towel and some dry clothes for him to put on afterwards. As guys go, he wasn't really that big, kind of average height, medium build, but he was bigger than I was, and I knew nothing of mine would fit him, even if he had been prepared to wear it. There was still some male clothing in the wardrobe in my mother's room. Though I had considered it often, I hadn't cleared out her stuff, and her room was pretty much as she'd left it, but tidied, her things neatly packed away, as if she'd gone travelling on a ticket with an open-date return and might come back at any moment. I even changed the bedding every couple of months, though I couldn't say why. It was just me here, and while I often passed time in her room, I never slept in my mother's bed, ever.

Inside her wardrobe I found a dressing gown, maroon with paisley trim, and I took it back to the bathroom with the towel. The door was still ajar, and though I knocked first, I found him stepping out of his underclothes as I entered.

He turned around to face me, making no effort to cover himself. The bathroom light was on and its bright glare permitted neither shadow nor softening. Though only in his fifties, he was headed towards an old man's body: thin and hairy, and gnarled like a cherry tree. His pubic hair was thick and grey. His penis flaccid. I could smell his body above the hot bath steam: moist stale sweat, tobacco and rum. He nodded his thanks for the clothes, turned his back to me and stepped into the bath.

I heard him turn the taps off as I picked up his wet clothing from the floor, and as he lay back and closed his eyes I backed out of the bathroom, pulling the door shut behind me.

*

By the time Lemon came downstairs dinner was ready. Minted couscous, grilled salmon and cherry tomatoes, with spring onions, black olives and yellow peppers tastefully strewn across two large white plates. The dressing gown was knotted tightly around his waist, and his pale legs carried him soundlessly across the living-room floor.

'You hungry?' I asked.

He shrugged. 'You have anything to drink?'

I indicated the bottle of wine on the table, but he shook his head.

'Water? Juice? Strong?'

'Strong's good.'

'Help yourself. Cupboard under the microwave. Glasses are above the sink.'

In my mother's day, unless she was entertaining, the double doors at the end of the through-lounge were always kept locked, so that you had to go out into the passage to enter the kitchen. But I kept them open always, and he went through to the kitchen. I heard him opening cupboards, finding the things he needed. He'd always been good in the kitchen; tidy and able. I only just made out the sound of the fridge door closing and I shivered.

Most things, all they want is a little gentle handling.

I refilled my own glass for the second time from the bottle on the table, sipping this one slowly as I waited for him to return. When he did, he was clutching a tumbler filled with a clear liquid that was probably vodka, diluted with water perhaps, or perhaps not. I picked up my fork and began to eat as he sat down and took a couple of glugs from the glass in his hand. I saw him wince as if he felt the liquor burn on the way down. He glanced at me, read the question in my eyes, and briefly waved a hand in my direction, dismissing it as nothing.

His knuckles were bigger than I recalled, or maybe they just seemed bigger because they were so clumsy wielding the knife and fork as he grasped them tight and started poking around the food on his plate, investigating, unhappy. After a while, he looked at me and asked, 'Ah wah dis?'

My laughter caught me by surprise. He had come to England when he was still in his twenties, had lived here some thirty years since, and normally spoke slowly, his English tinged with a distinctly Caribbean drawl. He was from Montserrat; a small islander. That he had chosen to ask what I was feeding him in that way was an indication of the level of his disgust.

'If you were expecting dasheen and curry goat you've come to the wrong place.'

'I never expect that, but little gravy would be good.'

'You should taste it,' I said, as he pushed the plate away from him into the centre of the table, shaking his head.

'You want some pepper?'

He shook his head again.

I carried on eating. He liked the brown food; brown rice, brown chicken, brown macaroni cheese, brown roast potatoes, the kind of food my mother was so good at cooking, the kind of food I never prepared.

'My wife died,' he said.

'Did she?'

'Cancer. Five months back.'

'I'm sorry.'

'Wasn't ill or nothing. Just couldn't eat. Lost some weight. Went to the doctor's. Doctor send her straight to the hospital. They open her, look inside, then sew her back up. Wasn't nothing they could do.'

He swallowed a mouthful from his glass, closed his eyes as it went down, then took another quick swig. He dabbed the sleeve of the dressing gown delicately against the corners of his mouth as if he were using a napkin. He would have seen her hollowed out, skeletal, with even her gums shrunken so her dentures no longer fit. They would have used wax to plump her cheeks out, to give her mouth a fuller, more natural shape, and a transparent liquid tint to make her skin tone lifelike. In the right hands she would have looked healthier dead than when he'd last seen her alive. Though I knew he was married, I had never met his wife.

'What was her name?'

'Mavis.'

'What was she like?'

He shrugged. 'I took care of her myself. Never put her in no home or nothing. Had to give up my job and everything. Couldn't manage both.' He raised his glass again, this time to sip. 'Must be the first time I touch her, she fall pregnant. Her mum was gonna chuck her out in the street and she never had no place else to go. Must be three months from I meet her, sex her, baby on the way, and we done married off already.'

'Did you love her?' The words were out in the open before I'd even realized they'd been in my mind. It was the question

7

I had wanted to ask him when I was sixteen years old. All this time it had waited, as intact as if it had been embalmed, buried deep inside my memory banks, and I hadn't had a clue.

'Baby was on the way so fast, and she was sick, sick and vomiting till the boy born. Bills was coming like mountain chicken after rainstorm, one after the next after the next. Never had time to roll on a beach, or check a dance till dawn. Never really laugh much...hardly smile. But at the end, I was there for her. Cooked her pumpkin soup. I feed her from the spoon and wipe her chin. I change her nappy and clean her mess. I did that.'

'Did she love you?' I asked.

For a moment, he did not respond. When he shrugged it was as if he considered the question irrelevant. He said, 'She let me stay.'

It was my turn to share, to present my life's summary. His turn to ask random, intimate questions. I waited but he asked nothing. Finally, 'I have a son now,' I said.

Lemon looked around the room slowly, taking in the alcoved shelves filled with books, the comfy wicker chair beside them, the settee that ran the length of one wall, the stereo in front of the window, the TV on the stand above it. There were no toys to be seen. Nothing to indicate that anyone other than me lived here. I had photos but they were not displayed like fertility trophies on my walls.

'He lives with his dad,' I said too quickly. 'He's coming tomorrow. Comes every second weekend and stays.'

He nodded, then stared back down at his glass without the slightest curiosity. I was relieved. I was always braced for the automatic surprise to that statement, the judging people did of me, their revision of everything they thought they knew about me before, like knowing that one fact put me as an individual into context. He hadn't done that and I was glad. In all the years he'd been away, there were some things that hadn't changed. People always felt they could trust him. That had always been his gift.

'So is that why you came?'

He looked up, eyes narrowed, brow furrowed. I had lost him.

'Because of Mavis.'

He smiled sadly, and shook his head.

'We never talked,' he said. 'About you mum and all that.'

Though I knew we would talk about her, that it was inevitable she would come up, I panicked, standing up even though I hadn't finished eating, reaching for his plate, scraping the untouched contents on to mine, gathering together the cutlery and placing it on top.

'She's been dead for years. It's over,' I said.

'Is it?' he asked, then looked away, down at the floor, wriggling his toes as he spoke, alternate feet tapping the floor like the hands of a drummer sounding a beat. My heart began to pound, the wine spun inside my head and from nowhere nausea rose inside my stomach like a buoy.

'Berris came to look for me,' he said, then added, 'He's out.'

I did the washing-up. Then wiped down the cupboards and the worktop. I cleaned the cooker, emptied the bin, then swept and mopped the kitchen floor.

Lemon was in the living room. Smoking. I could smell it. It was something I had forgotten, the smoking. Him and Berris had both smoked back then and burned incense over it. Benson & Hedges and the occasional spliff. My mother had provided the incense. She had never been a smoker herself. The only other man she'd ever lived with was my father and he hadn't smoked either. Yet, like everything else, she accepted it without a murmur, throwing the windows wide, pinning the curtains back, waving the joss stick around in circles. I closed my eyes and for a second I saw her: small and slim and perfect, arms raised, dancing.

He's out.

He had served fourteen years of a life sentence, a fixed-term punishment with rules and walls that had now ended, and I envied him. Able to begin his life anew, his crime atoned for in full. Blamed and punished, he had served his time, then been freed. Free to visit Lemon so the two of them could talk. Now Lemon was here to talk to me. I inhaled deeply, leaning against the wall, eyes closed, willing myself to calm down, unable to stop the question echoing inside my head: how much did Lemon already know?

I took a saucer from the cupboard and carried it back into the living room. He'd been using his hand, his cupped palm, to flick the ash into.

'I don't have an ashtray. I don't smoke,' I said, handing him the saucer.

He was sitting in the middle of the settee. I moved to the wicker chair opposite and sat there, watching him, waiting for him to speak. He held the cigarette pinched between forefinger and thumb, took a long, slow drag and opened his mouth to allow some of the smoke to curl lazily upward into his nostrils, before finally drawing it down into his lungs. As he blew out, his rounded lips shaped the smoke into rings and he pulsed them out, one after the next, till the smoke was gone.

The nausea from earlier was still there, like my mother was being exhumed, and in the silence it was getting worse. I was desperate to know what he knew, yet at the same time petrified he would blurt it out before I was ready. It was that fear which drove me to speak first, to start the conversation from the outside edge, the farthest point away from the core that I could find.

'So how'd he look?'

'He's changed.'

I raised my eyebrows, looked up at the ceiling and pursed my lips to contain a snort.

'Don't believe it if you want, but it's true.'

'I've heard that before...'

'He's not the only one.'

I felt the familiar stirring of anger, and I embraced it. Had he expected to find me the same after all this time, after all that had happened? 'I've grown up,' I said. He didn't respond. Instead he concentrated on putting the cigarette out. 'So what did he want?'

'To say thanks for me being his friend.'

'How touching.'

'And he asked after you.'

'Ahh...sweet.'

'And to say sorry.'

'Fuck him!'

Lemon raised his eyebrows. His was the old-school generation. It was all right for them to *rass claat* and *pussy claat*
and *bomba claat*, but children were expected to be seen and
not heard. Even though I was an adult in my own right, I was
still a clear generation younger than him. He considered my
swearing disrespectful.

'It's a bit late for apologies,' I said.

'It's never too late to try and undo the wrong a man's
done.'

'That's rubbish and I don't want to hear it! She's dead.'

'I take it you're without sin?'

Though there was no suggestion of sarcasm in his tone,
I felt myself struggling to read between the lines, trying hard
to gauge what he knew; flailing. 'I don't need any belated
apologies from him. Or lectures from *you* on sin.'

'That's not why I came.'

'So why did you come? What is it you want?'

He looked away from me, down at the floor. Now it felt
like I was pressuring him, but it was already too late for me
to stop.

'He cried, didn't he? I bet he bawled his eyes out. He was
always good at that.'

'He wasn't the only one.'

'And you listened and nodded and said, "I forgive you"?'

He didn't answer. Nor did he look at me.

This time I made no effort to hold the snort back. 'I need a
drink,' I said.

I went back into the kitchen, took another glass from the cupboard and filled it with more wine I did not want. My heart was pounding inside my chest, my throat dry; the hatred I had spent so many years suppressing was back with a thud as hard-hitting as a train. All the walls, the structure, the neatness of my life, and he'd smashed through them with two words casually tossed.

He's out.

I left the wine untouched and stormed back inside the living room.

'You know what, I don't want you here,' I said. 'You'd better go.'

And he said, 'Not yet.'

'You just don't get it, do you? I don't care that she's dead!'

He didn't even glance my way, merely shrugged. 'And me? I never gave a damn that she live.'

I had been running for the last four years. It had come upon me one day, a few weeks after Red had left me. I hadn't worked since I was six months pregnant. That probably had a lot to do with it, because when I was working I was *feeling*. Outside of the cold room, I felt nothing. That particular day, I had finished repainting my bedroom white. It had been cream when I'd started, cream and burgundy, because Red hated white. He said it was sterile, that he wanted to be comfortable kicking off his boots in the bedroom, to feel cosy and warm. Once he had gone, I had no further need for compromise, so I changed it.

I had thought that when it was finished I would feel something; satisfaction or pleasure, even uncertainty or dislike, *anything*, but I didn't. The job was finished, that was all. It was done. I washed the brushes, cleaned out the bathtub, packed the cans away into the garden shed and went upstairs to look at my handiwork again. My relationship had ended and Red had taken my son. My life was my own and I could do anything I wanted, yet I felt nothing. As I stood staring at the walls, searching inside myself for some kind of emotional response, the nothingness suddenly welled up inside me, like a physical mass, so vast and empty and infinite I was terrified. The very first time I went running, it was from that terror, from the possibility of being sucked down into emptiness for ever, and as I ran I discovered I *was* able to feel; pressure in my lungs, pain in my legs, my skin perspiring, the pounding of my heart.

My routine was erratic, I ran when I felt like it, usually five or six times a month. So was my style. It was nothing like that of the runners I grew accustomed to seeing, the ones who regulated themselves, jogged two or three times a week, who did a warm-up first and stretching exercises afterwards, the people for whom the activity was a hobby. I ran like my life depended on it, as fast and as hard as I could. Sometimes, passers-by would look beyond me as I ran towards them, with fear in their eyes, trying to see who or what was pursuing me, trying to work out whether they should be running too. As long as I was feeling, I didn't care.

But that night, with Lemon smoking in the living room, my mother dancing in the kitchen and Berris out, it felt like my circuits were overloaded. I found myself feeling too much at once to be able to process any of it, and the only thing I could think to do was run.

I left him sitting on the settee, pulled on jogging bottoms and trainers and took off. The moment I closed the garden gate behind me, my feet began pummelling the pavement and I found myself headed towards Hackney Downs in a sprint.

I turned right at the park, intending to follow its perimeter, and raced along Downs Park Road, with the park on my left and the Pembury housing estate on my right. The evening was as dark as night, the weather drizzling again and windy. Icy cold.

I felt it.

Felt the breath in my throat like pure eucalyptus, the liquid droplets in the air against my face and neck, my calf muscles screaming. I focused with all my might on the things I could physically feel, hoping to cork the memories Lemon had stirred up about a time I had no desire to remember, and it worked for about twenty minutes, till I had run more than halfway around Hackney Downs. Defeat came in the form of a piece of paper, a mere scrap, tossed on a wind to land against my hand with a wet slap. I flicked it off immediately and increased my speed, but it was already too late. Suddenly it was impossible not to think of her, my mother, and the choices she had made, to wonder how any woman could ever be so pathetic, could become so weak and passive that she would not raise her own hand to defend herself, even in the final moments when she must have known that if she didn't she would surely die.

*

Too beautiful. Everyone said she was and it was true. With baby-wide eyes and long thick lashes in a perpetual flirt-flutter, and purple-blush lips that parted in a half-moon over even ivory teeth, and high colour so flawless it was as if she had been slow-dipped in a vat of chestnut gloss, lowered and turned and raised by a patient doll-maker, his hands clenched tight around the ebony mass of her kink-free coolie hair – my mother had been a beauty.

She was the only child of a poor, uneducated Montserratian land worker and his semi-literate wife. In an era when it was normal for Caribbean migrants to leave their children behind with relatives as they headed out to the Motherland to make their fortune, with the wild card Hope flapping hard against the ribcage, my grandparents took their daughter with them. Between the three of them, they bore a single cardboard grip, and most of what was inside it belonged to her. Everything I know about them I learned from her, and the sum of everything she said was that they could not have worshipped God himself more than they worshipped the ground she walked on. Full stop.

She was too beautiful to make her own way to and from school at a time when every other child in the country was doing it, or to cook or clean or shop or carry, or even to amass a single useful life skill. So when she was seventeen and my grandparents died, it is hard to imagine what would have become of her were it not for the benevolence of my grandfather's friend Mr Jackson.

Mr Jackson was fifty-three when he took her in. *Fifty-three.* Fair with the tenants who rented the rooms in his house, he was a shrewd Jamaican migrant who had somehow landed soundly on his rickety old legs. He was gaunt from the diabetes that would eventually finish him off for good, and though half blind from glaucoma he still had vision enough to see that my mother was too beautiful to weep broken-hearted, forlorn in her single bed, *alone*.

Within a year, they were married and she was rescued. It was Mr Jackson who taught her how to be a woman, how to pick good vegetables, the best pieces of meat to buy, how to cut chicken, gut fish, where to shop for everything you needed to make a jug of Guinness Punch.

He took her shopping. Bought her jewellery and underwear, dresses and jackets and shoes that she chopped and changed like a child with a dressing-up box and nothing to do but play. She was too beautiful for anything but the very best and that was all she had because Mr Jackson doted on her.

My mother talked about herself all the time, told me everything about her life as though she were telling fairy tales, talking while she played with my hair or I played with hers, whispering in my ear as she tucked me into bed at night, or on cold nights in her bed as I snuggled into her warmth. About her and my father, how they had been married nearly three years before conceiving me, how by then he'd lost all hope of ever fathering a child. When my mother told him she was expecting, he was both overjoyed and convinced I would be a boy. It was Mr Jackson who called me the name they went on to enter into the *Register of Births and Deaths*, as if it were a real name they had given a lot of thought to, a normal name, borne of love. He said it suited me, not just a girl, but one who, instead of looking like his wife, resembled *him*; small and dark and demanding, too greedy for my mother to keep on the breast, too noisy for my father to want in their bedroom. After I arrived, he gave up the tenants and bought the house I still lived in, with a bedroom for them, one for me, and a third just in case, then kept me and my mother locked up tight inside it. Away from church and work and parties and shebeens and hard-assed younger men and life.

She whiled away a few more years till Mr Jackson died, cheating me of all memory of him bar one: me sitting on the bed beside him, rapt, listening as he told me a story. What it was about, I do not know. I can barely see him in the memory or recall any detail of the room. The most vivid thing I remember was my excitement, the sheer thrill I felt listening as he spoke. I must have been about three. By the time I was four he was gone.

I had completed a full circuit of the park and was too shattered to run the rest of the way home, so I power-walked, on shaking legs, past the estate and the garages, past the houses and gardens of normal families, back to where I knew Lemon waited. I opened the garden gate and, at the front door, felt my left calf beginning to cramp, so stopped and stretched it, trying to stave off the worst of the pains.

The one thing my mother always said about Mr Jackson was that he was a decent man, that he took proper care of things, including this mortgage-free house that he left to her, which she then left to me when I was sixteen and she was dead. Decent enough to ask no more of her than that she occupy it and dedicate her life to raising me, forsaking all other men till I had grown up. 'Grown up' she interpreted to mean when I was sixteen. It was ironic that I actually *had* grown up then. Sixteen and overnight my childhood was over.

Maybe everything that happened was Mr Jackson's fault. Had he married someone his own age, he might not have been so obsessed with the idea of other men sleeping with his wife after he was gone. Maybe had she had the chance to live in the real world, she would have picked up a few strategies to stop it killing her. Or maybe if I'd been given a name like Peace, it would have been a self-fulfilling prophecy of a different kind.

But I was making excuses and I knew it. The fact was, I had done what I had done. Made up my own mind and committed myself to a course of action. My blame was my blame and my blame alone. I opened the front door and entered the house, then slammed it shut behind me, as if in doing so it was possible to lock a world's worth of excuses outside it.

Inside the shower cubicle I scrubbed. Scrubbed my arms and legs, my neck, stomach and breasts. The scent of bergamot shower gel had begun to subside, and my skin reddened in response to what had become an abrasive rub till, eventually, it began to sting. I stopped scrubbing then, standing beneath the coursing water till the hot water went warm, then tepid, then cool, and the sting became a tingle and goosebumps swelled. I withstood the cold till I could bear it no longer, before finally turning the water off.

I slid open the glass door, reaching for the white thick-pile bath towel, becoming gentler with my aching body, slowly patting it dry. With the towel wrapped around me, I unlocked the bathroom door and stepped out on to the landing, headed towards my bedroom. As I passed my mother's room, the door was slightly ajar. I paused outside it, listening to the silence within before slowly pushing it open and entering.

Inside her room there was a cupboard full of coats. The cupboard had been built into the alcove and was probably as old as the house itself. I went over and creaked open the door. The coats were suspended inside it on large wooden hangers, each one an expensive and beautiful work of fine tailoring, protected individually by transparent dustcovers. I ran my fingers across the tops of the hangers lightly before settling on one, which I then withdrew.

Carefully I raised the cover and examined the coat underneath. It was made from nubuck suede, a long, ankle-length, close-fitting garment, grey-blue like cloudy sky, with diagonal slit pockets lined in cobalt-coloured silk.

A gift.

A small tug, a dulled pop, the button was forced through the hole and the coat was off the hanger. I pushed my arms into the sleeves and stepped out of the towel nest around my feet. Deeply, eyes closed, I inhaled the stale scent of years infused with leather. A surreal dizziness mushroomed inside my head and I swayed slightly, then surfed the remainder of its wave.

I did up every button. My body was a little fuller than hers and the coat moulded my naked shape as perfectly as a second skin.

I walked to the mirror where I examined myself, turning this way and that, moving my legs to emphasize the long slits at the buttonless bottom of the front and the vented back. I studied my reflection side on, unhappy. I sat on the stool before the dressing table, pulled my damp hair up into a ponytail, picked up her brush and a powder foundation, and started dusting it on.

This was the one thing she had taught me to do well, applying make-up with such proficiency I could even make the dead look like they were dozing. She had let me brush her powder on, allowed me to practise coating her long lashes in sooty mascara, her full lips in glossy plums, while she sat hardly blinking, still as a doll. She had preferred Max Factor, and as I used up the items on her dressing table I replaced them with the same, though for my workbag I chose an assortment of brands that were just as effective on brown skins.

Apart from the foundations, her other cosmetics suited my colour as much as they had hers. I picked a red-bronze rouge, a golden eyeshadow, and painted my lips a metallic mocha brown. Finished, I examined my reflection again, still dissatisfied, knowing the picture was incomplete. I pulled my hair out of the ponytail, pushed my fingertips beneath the surface, down to the scalp, and tousled it from the roots to create more body. I pulled the sides and back up, leaving the top mussy and wild, and held the glamorous style in place with one hand.

I tilted my head slightly, exposing more of my neck, and mirrored in the glass I saw Lemon, just inside the bedroom door, and I froze, watching him watching me. He looked as shocked as if he had seen a ghost. My attention returned to my reflection where I expected to see myself posing, but instead, after all the years she'd been dead, I found myself face to face with my mother.

I gasped and stood up too quickly, knocking the stool over behind me, then tripping on it as I stepped back, releasing my hair and stumbling. I might have fallen but for Lemon who was inside the room now, close enough behind me that I could feel his heat. He grabbed my arm and held it firmly, steadying me. I turned around to ask whether he'd seen what I had, but when I looked at him, his eyes were as hotly fired as a kiln, and everything I had to say lodged as thickly inside my throat as grief.

'She was beautiful,' he said, slowly raising his hands and smoothing the sides of my hair, cocking his head as if to get a better angle for the view, smiling, but not at me, at something he saw in the distance. Some*one*. 'I never seen anyone as beautiful in my life.'

He held my head between his hands like a ball, moving only his thumbs, stroking my eyebrows from thick end to thin with a slow, hypnotic repetition.

'They have a rock down by Carr's Bay back home. Huge. 'Bout the size of a small house, off the beach, in the water, with some small rocks leading up to it, good size but small-looking alongside the big one; like a bridge. When you on top of the big one, it's like you out to sea. Most times the sea down there was rough, with big waves – if you was in the water could knock a man down clean.

'Don't exactly know how to describe it, when I used to climb out there and sit down, how I felt, 'cept "good". She was the only person to ever make me have that feeling on dry land. Just to look at her. That was all. Just to see.'

Leisurely, he ran his palms down my neck on both sides, thumbs around the front – if he changed mood they could strangle me – and out, across my shoulders, before returning to my neck. Then his hands moved downwards, over the front of the coat, tracing the swell of my breasts beneath the coat's peach-skin nap. I stepped back.

'No,' I said.

It was his turn to step back. He sat down on the edge of the bed and looked around the room, the floor, the walls, everywhere but at me.

'She wore that coat that night,' he said.

'I know.'

'She was looking out for him the whole night and I was looking at her, feeling like I was on the rock, thinking what a fool he was, knowing he was still but a small fool compared to me, the Fool King.'

So much time had passed since then, almost a decade and a half, yet the details were all there, as vivid as if everything had happened only yesterday.

'He was so angry,' I said.

Lemon nodded. 'I knew he would be.'

'I couldn't talk to him,' but even as I said the words I knew that was not the truth of it. I had not spoken when I should have done, and then when I did, I had lied.

'He woulda never listen. Not them times. Kinda man he was then.'

I pushed hard and the words tumbled out of my mouth. 'I didn't think about her; just me.'

'You was young. You was scared.'

It was the compassion in his voice that made me bristle, the understanding. 'How the hell would you know? You weren't there!'

'You're right,' he said. 'I wasn't.'

'No one was! So don't you ever try and tell me how I felt because I am the only person who knows.'

I turned my back to him and started unbuttoning the coat. Though my hands were shaking, I was impatient to be done. I knew now that he did not know. He was making excuses for the little he thought I was responsible for and he could not have done that if he had even the slightest inkling of the truth. But instead of relief, I felt disappointment. I had been let down. Again.

'We need to talk,' Lemon said. 'There's things I need to tell you. About me. What I done.'

'Save it for *Trisha*!' I answered, securing the towel around my body before taking the coat off. I retrieved the hanger from the bed and fed the coat back on to it, pulling down the cover, putting it back into its space inside the cupboard. 'She's got time and sympathy. Have you not noticed I'm a bit lacking on the touchy-feely front?'

'Yes,' he said, 'I have.'

Another day, different circumstances, and the sincerity of his voice to my rhetorical question might have made me smile. I had hoped he had known and had still come anyway.

It had to be him. He had always been the only person who might understand; my only hope.

'You can sleep in here,' I said. His eyes moved around the room, with its flower-patterned walls and old-fashioned furnishings in sharp contrast to the other rooms in the house. I'd had to replace the original carpet because the stains had been impossible to remove. Otherwise, her bedroom had been as carefully preserved as a crypt. 'Unless you're scared of jumbies?'

He gave a single nod and suddenly I was exhausted.

'My son's coming in the morning,' I said. 'You're gonna have to give me space. I can't do that and...this. It's too much.'

He nodded again.

'My son comes first,' I said and felt a blush rising. I wondered why I had added those words and whether he had seen through them. 'I'll see you in the morning,' I said, and left.

2

They arrived at ten on the dot, punctual as ever. Red rang the doorbell once and Ben banged the flap of the letter box over and over again non-stop, up until the actual moment I opened the front door. To hear him you would have thought there was some kind of emergency, that it was urgent he get inside, that maybe having had no contact with me since his last visit a fortnight ago, he was desperate to see me again. Yet the instant I opened the door he became shy, twirling one finger round and round inside his mouth, leaning against Red, the other hand wrapped around his father's long leg as though it were a life-support system. Ben looked down at the floor, stealing glances at me with those huge eyes and thick dark lashes he'd inherited from my mother. Red nudged him with his knee.

'Aren't you going to say hello to your mum?'

Without taking the finger out he said, 'Hello, Jinx.'

I bent down and picked him up, cuddling him clumsily, trying to ignore his passive resistance as I kissed him yet irritated by it;

hardly one step through the door and he was already being difficult. He was clean, shiny as a new chestnut, and I inhaled deeply the smell of the cocoa butter on his skin and the coconut oil rubbed into his hair, sweet and at the same time cloying.

'Hello, little man,' I said and kissed his cheek.

'Urgh.' He wiped the kiss off. 'I hate lipstick.'

I laughed as if he were joking and kissed him again. 'You'll love it when you're older.'

'When I'm older,' he asked, 'will you be dead?'

Though there was nothing in his tone but interest, the question floored me completely. Stunned, I opened my mouth to reply, but could think of nothing to say.

'The mum of one of the kids in Ben's class is dead,' Red said, his tone neutral. 'Ever since he found out, he's been obsessed.'

'Will you?' Ben pressed.

'Mummy will die when she's old,' his father answered, and I had to bite my tongue, because I knew better than anyone that death did not pre-book appointments decades in advance. Its approach was random, based on whimsy, often violent. I came from a line of women who bore a single child and were dead before its eighteenth birthday. 'You've got nothing to worry about,' Red said.

I turned and carried Ben into the living room, giving Red an eyeful of my bared legs. I had been up for hours after sleeping badly, head full, muscles aching. My legs were freshly shaved and creamed from the heel up to the high hemline of the fitted black skirt I had worn for his benefit, so short that it was a wonder it covered the icebox he believed hummed between my legs. I heard the squeaky friction of his trainer soles against the flooring as he followed me in.

'So how *is* school?' I asked my son. He would be five next month, had started school last week. It was incredible to me that his nursery days were at an end when I was still getting over his birth. He was growing up fast, getting heavy. I put him down.

'Okay,' he said, twisting and bending his head and shoulders and hips in a writhe.

I looked up at Red. Even in my heels he was still a clear foot taller than me. Smelling of shower gel and aftershave and skin cream freshly applied. He was dressed casually in a tracksuit, hands tucked deep inside the pockets of his trousers. His body language was, as always, relaxed. It was one of the first things that had attracted me to him, the perfect proportions of his body, the grace in his movements, the flawless lines.

We had met over his father's corpse after he had died from a stroke, his face contorted. I had spent the day working on him: inserting eye caps to close his eyes, small pieces of foam in his cheeks to recreate symmetry, suturing his upper and lower jaws to bring his lips together naturally, then using a mouth-former to fix them in a position inclined towards a smile. I had shaved him and trimmed his hair, and applied a layer of make-up that was virtually imperceptible but restored his colour and gave his cheeks a healthy flush.

I had almost finished dressing him when Red returned to view him in his casket. Having been the person who had discovered the body, he'd had to brace himself hard against seeing his father again to say goodbye. When he saw what I had done, he was speechless, just stood there staring down at his father for the longest time, then finally cried. Days later, he told me he had been too horrified to cry when he had found his father. The tears he'd shed in the parlour had been sheer relief. Laid out, his father not only looked dapper, but also completely at peace.

I had been attracted to Red straight away. Grief-stricken, with his height and grace and raw vulnerability, to me he was irresistible. It was ironic that the same things I'd been attracted to, now made me feel mocked.

'Is he settling down okay?' I asked.

'Yeah. Fine. You should've phoned him. He would've told you himself.' His tone was even for Ben's benefit. 'School was good.' His voice became gentler as he stepped over to stand beside Ben, rubbing his enormous hand over the small boy's skiffled head. This was where he always won, hands down. He was a good dad. Naturally good.

'You were *so* grown up, weren't you? Come on, gimmee a hug. I've got to go.'

'I wanna come with you,' Ben's voice was tiny. He glanced up at me as though he would have preferred it if I wasn't listening.

'Come on, don't start that again. We've talked about this, haven't we? Your mum *wants* to spend time with you...' – he threw an angry glance at me – '...and I'll be back to get you tomorrow.'

'But I'm not feeling well. My tummy hurts. Feel my head.'

Red put his hand on Ben's head. 'You're not hot. You'll be fine.'

'I wanna come with you, *please*, Daddy...'

He stooped to hug his son tight, to kiss him, and I watched Ben's desperate response, claw-cuddling, kissing *him* back, trying to lift his legs from the floor to force Red into picking him up.

'Come on,' I said, going over and lifting Ben up myself. 'Your dad has to go. He has things to do.' I imagined they involved another woman, on her back, legs wide, wet. 'We're gonna have fun.' My smile felt tight.

Ben stopped struggling, resigning himself to my hip and his staying. His lower lip trembled.

'You've got my number. Any problems, ring,' Red said. 'I'll pick him up tomorrow about four.'

'Fine,' I answered.

A moment later I heard the metallic click of the front door as it closed behind him and, simultaneously, Ben began to cry.

He didn't want to eat or drink or watch TV or play. He followed me around like a dog, not speaking or interacting, with a wretched expression on his face as if his small shoulders bore the weight of the world in grief.

On my part I made small talk, trying to engage him in a conversation of some kind: *How's school? Do you have many friends? Are they nice? Would you like me to make you something to eat? Please tell me, is your mouth going to stay like that for the rest of the day?* Often his reply was a single word consisting of just the one syllable. Occasionally it was not even that, just a nod or a shake of the head. It was as exhausting trying to get a conversation going as giving birth itself. He had only been with me an hour when I found myself working out that it would be twenty-nine hours more before his dad came back to collect him.

So far, Lemon had slept through everything. There had been no sounds from upstairs, no indication he planned to get out of bed at any time today, but the fact he was here, the things he had stirred, the *feelings*, put me under more pressure than usual, which I hadn't realized was even possible. Since Lemon had arrived, I'd found myself engaged on some kind of voyage of discovery. The failure of my relationship with Ben was something I simply accepted. I had no friends to speak of, there was no family to visit on my side, there were no observers. But with Lemon here, after my silly boast about Ben's needs being my top priority, I felt ashamed, as though for the first time I was on the outside of our relationship looking in, trying to gauge how it might appear to someone else, and from that perspective, things looked pretty grim indeed.

'I know,' I said, 'let's go out and do something.'

Though I wanted to change into something less dressy and maybe head for the park, I was reluctant to go back upstairs. I didn't want to wake Lemon just yet, or to introduce him to Ben while he was looking so unhappy, accusing me with his expression alone of being the world's worst mum.

So I decided to do something with him I didn't need to change for, and also that he would enjoy. Something nice together, something different, something fun.

'You've never been to the cinema before, have you?' I asked.

He shook his head.

'In that case, you'd better hurry and put your coat on. You're in for a real treat.'

We drove to the Rio on Kingsland High Street where, luckily, some kids' film or other was just starting, so we quickly bought popcorn and Coke and sweets, then hurried into the cinema before we had missed too much of the beginning to be able to follow the storyline.

He wanted to sit in the very front row and as I was determined not to spoil the occasion, I conceded. There, he faffed and fiddled, picking up his drink every fifteen seconds for a sip, putting it back down, then somehow finding yet more reasons to continue fidgeting. He stared around behind him regularly, as though the people sitting there were more interesting than what was on the screen in front of us, and asked a hundred questions about what was going on in the film, every one of which, had he been paying proper attention, he would have known the answers to himself. Finally, after about twenty minutes, he needed to go to the toilet.

'What, *now*?' I asked.

'Yessss,' he moaned, 'I can't hold it.'

We had to leave our seats, disturbing everyone else in the process, and crossed the foyer with me trying to explain that he shouldn't wait till the last minute to ask for the toilet, but should mention it in good time so it was not an actual emergency to get him there. As I spoke he was doing what looked like some kind of monkey dance, legs bowed wide, one hand cupped over his crotch, index finger and thumb in a pinch, as if he was holding the end of an inflated balloon and was trying to stop the air inside from escaping.

At the women's toilets I opened the door and stood waiting for him to enter.

'What's the matter?'

'I don't go in the girls' toilets,' he said, 'I go in the boys'.'

'We're not going into the men's,' I said.

'My daddy doesn't take me in the girls'.'

'I'm not your dad. I'm your mum and I'm not allowed in the men's toilets. We don't have a choice.'

'I can go on my own.'

'No you can't.'

He began to cry. 'I'm a boy,' he said.

'It's just a toilet, Ben!'

'But I go in the boys' toilets with Daddy.'

'Well, he's not here so you can't,' I said.

He didn't move, so I picked him up, ignoring the tears. Then he wriggled and howled as I carried him in, wrestled him into a cubical and undid his trousers. After he had emptied his bladder there was wee all around the seat and on the floor. There was even a little spray on the walls. I cleared up, then coerced him over to the sink so we could both wash our hands.

Outside in the foyer I had to calm him down because he was making too much noise for us to go back into the cinema. Even then, when we went back inside and took our seats, he was still sniffing, but mercifully subdued and quiet enough for us to be able to carry on watching what remained of the film. But just as I had begun to relax and think it might yet all come good still, he began to cry again.

'What is it?' I asked.

He shook his head.

'Shush! People are trying to watch the film. What on earth are you crying for now?'

His response was to cry yet louder. I stood up.

'Come on,' I said, but he shook his head. Other people in the cinema had had enough of us and were making their feelings known. I had no choice but to lift him up, put him on my hip and carry the reluctant boy out. As I put him down in the foyer, I felt the wetness of my skirt against my hip, then saw the telltale patch on the crotch of his pants.

'I can't believe you've wet yourself,' I said. 'This is bloody ridiculous!'

'I'm sorry, Jinx,' he said, and to his credit he did actually look as though he felt bad. But I was too far gone to be able to respond to his belated remorse.

'Don't give me that!' I shouted. 'I *know* you did it on purpose!'

Ben didn't speak to me on the drive home. He stared out of the passenger window all the way so that even when I could bring myself to glance at him from time to time, there was nothing for me to see but the back of his head.

I was angry, not just with him, and the wet pants, and the whole disaster of the trip, but with the entire and complete fiasco of our relationship. I felt like I was always a hair's breadth away from losing it with him, like I was out of control, like the capacity to hate and hurt was bigger inside me than any capacity to nurture. Instead of loving him, I was messing up his head. He would grow up to be the thing I wanted least for my son: to be like me. But though this was crystal clear, I did not know how to change it. It felt like something needed to happen inside me. But I was not a magician. There was no quick-fix abracadabra available to change me into anybody else.

At the traffic lights by the junction of Amhurst Road and Shacklewell Lane, in a car that pulled up alongside me while we idled waiting for amber, there was a woman with two young kids in the back, and she was pulling faces in the mirror and laughing with her offspring, and they were happy back. Though I couldn't hear a word of the exchange between them, it was not necessary. It was so obvious, her pleasure in them, in being with them; she was beaming. Her car was full of happy family sounds that I could only imagine. And I was jealous. I wanted what she had for myself.

My fortnightly sessions with Ben were a chore, a series of exasperations that drove me to despair. They always made me feel like I was on a treadmill pounding away without making the slightest iota of progress. And I hated it. Hated it all, the false hope, the wasted energy, the inevitability of failure it presented every time.

He could not get out of the car fast enough when I pulled up outside my house. Still tangled up inside the seat belt, stumbling in his haste, he leapt for freedom the moment I turned the ignition off. Then he ran up the garden path. By the time

I caught up with him he had ripped three or four heads off the crocuses planted along the thin bed that ran the length of the path from the gate to the front door.

'Ben, don't do that please,' I said as he started tearing off another. Ignoring me, he yanked it off anyway, adding it to the collection in his other hand.

'Will you bloody stop!' I said.

When he looked at me, those enormous eyes were filled with tears. He held out his hand. His voice was tiny. 'These are for you,' he said.

And I looked at the small, fresh, squashed bouquet held out to me, and for a second I could have taken his gift and smiled, then cuddled and whispered to my son, *Forgive me. I love you.*

But the words that came out of my mouth instead were: 'Great! Why don't you kill every single flower you can see?' And I looked away, into my handbag, searching for the keys as he opened his hand and let them fall, then rubbed his palms together to dry them.

I opened the front door and held it wide for him to enter, following him inside and closing it behind me with a deep sigh. He walked into the living room, stopped, gasped, then looked at me. I passed him. Inside the room, Lemon was sitting on the settee where he had been watching TV. He was wearing his trousers and a string vest, with the maroon dressing gown slung casually over the lot. He looked comfortable. *Too* comfortable.

'I forgot to say, Ben, I've got a friend staying with me.'

'Is he your boyfriend?' Ben asked.

'No, he's...' – *my man friend* is what came to mind – '...a family friend. Lemon, this is Ben.'

'Howdy,' Lemon said to Ben, slowly scratching his head with a single forefinger.

'Hello, Uncle Lemon,' Ben replied in the monotone of a child answering the class register, and I wondered who had taught him that old-fashioned rule, to call adults 'Uncle' or 'Auntie' out of respect, and whether he had begun that lesson by calling some woman 'Auntie' in his father's home.

Lemon held his hand out and Ben took and shook it. Then he started to laugh.

'Hey! Who give you joke?' Lemon asked.

'Lemon's a funny name.'

'That's for sure.'

'I don't like lemons. When I lick them my eyes go squeezy squeezy.'

'Next time, dip it in sugar first. Then taste.'

'Is that how *you* eat them?'

'Always.'

'Lemon likes lemons,' Ben said and laughed again.

Lemon looked at me. 'I see there's more than one comedian in the family,' he said.

Though I could not think of a single joke I had cracked with Lemon, I gave him a tight smile and answered, 'So it seems.'

Ben walked over to the settee and was about to sit down. 'Come on, Ben. You need to come upstairs with me so I can change you.'

'Are you going now?' Ben asked.

'Not as far as I know,' Lemon said. 'I'll be right hereso when you come back.'

Then, as if he had just been given the best news he had heard in a long, long time, like maybe his team had just scored the goal that would assure them the cup, Ben punched the air and grinned.

'Yeah!' he said.

If Lemon had been wearing a skirt, Ben would have been up underneath it. He followed Lemon around like he was a beloved relative who after having been missing for years and presumed dead, had miraculously been found alive and restored to the bosom of his family.

The two of them played with their lunch, chicken nuggets, ketchup and chips – the only meal Ben was guaranteed to eat a bit of – as if they were both five-year-olds. Lemon laughed his head off at everything Ben said and, inspired by this, Ben hardly paused between words for breath.

I listened as he told Lemon about Max in his class whose front tooth came out when he bit into the apple in his packed lunch. There were anecdotes about his Power Ranger toys, Thomas the Tank Engine, and Shaggy's exploits in *Scooby-Doo*. He talked about his new teacher, Mrs Smith, and how impressed she was with his reading. Lemon gave him a piece of paper and a pen and Ben proved once and for all that he could write his name himself without any help from anyone.

I was in shock. I had never heard my son like this before. I had simply thought he was a morose child, because morose was how he always was when he was with me. I had never seen this side of him, this laughing chattiness, the non-stop outpouring of everything going on in his life, the pleasure he took from his accomplishments, such as they were. And I felt hurt. Really hurt. Wounded to the core just listening to how natural and happy he could be with a virtual stranger, when I had been trying for nearly five years to have a relationship with him and had come up against brick after brick after brick.

He made me feel how he had made me feel when he was a baby. Like no matter what I did or how much time I put in or how hard I tried, anyone could walk into his life and they were immediately more important than I was. Like I did not matter. My existence meant nothing. And all the while, as I sat on the periphery of their conversation, I could feel myself getting angrier and angrier, and though I tried to rationalize my way out of it, I just couldn't stop myself.

So I left them to finish lunch together and I did more cleaning. Upstairs, I entered the smallest room of the house, Ben's. I had painted this room while I was pregnant, a pale yellow that had darkened over the years to a colour similar to the skin on a bowl of cold custard. I had chosen yellow because it was a perfect colour for a girl's room, and neutral enough in case the baby had been a boy. It contained a single bed covered in a yellow quilt, which ran the length of one wall, a small wardrobe and a tiny desk with drawers below. On top of the desk was Ben's bag for overnighting, his dirty clothes folded neatly beside it. A large car was parked in one corner, left behind when Red had left four years ago, too cumbersome to carry with them at the time, then just forgotten.

Since then, Ben had grown so much he could no longer fit inside it.

To be honest, there was nothing inside the room to clean. This was a space that merely needed the occasional airing. I had left my son downstairs and gone upstairs into his empty bedroom to connect with him. It was ridiculous, but true. I sat down on the bed and held my head in my hands. For the umpteenth time, I wished with all my might that things between me and my son were different, but they had been this way for ever.

I never wanted a boy. All the way through my pregnancy it was a daughter I prayed for. A living doll to dress up and cherish, who I could sing to and fuss over and love with abandon. Then along came Ben, after a difficult birth; two days' hard labour, episiotomy, forceps and suction cup, the boy had to be dragged from my body in a screeching, splitting, bloody gush, huge dark balls and willy in disproportion to the rest of his body.

Red was over the moon. As ecstatic as my father might have been had I been born a boy. He returned to the maternity suite that evening grinning and bearing a blue-ribboned bouquet of long-stemmed white lilies – my mother's favourite; flowers that would have been perfect for her grave.

But Ben wasn't fooled by any of this. For the first day he didn't feed, just lay there watching me, an unhappy frown creasing his dry, scaly brow, disapproving even then, as though he knew the numb, dumb shock I was going through was as much to do with him as the experience he had put me through, like he was already aware he couldn't count on me.

He had an air of resignation about him, acknowledging me as his biological mother and also, his certainty that I would eventually let him down. I wondered if he wanted to die.

The second day, as if some reasoning had altered the course of his mind, he started to cry, a shrill, angry catcall to feed, mouth opened wide to be filled with the breast and when I gave it to him he clamped down on it like a vice, not just drinking milk but consuming *me*, like some starved pygmy cannibal, sucking so hard I could have stood up and let go of him and he would have swung like a pit bull, suspended in mid-air by the sheer power of his jaws and the vacuum forcing my nipple deep down his throat.

Within days my tender flesh was reduced to raw, weeping meat and he had to go on the bottle. I harboured hopes then that with my body back I might begin the process of recovering, but no. If it wasn't hunger or nappy rash it was colic, night and day, unsettled and unhappy, he cried and cried and cried, calming down only in his father's arms, sleeping only on his father's chest, rejecting me so completely the only thing I felt was resentment.

That was when the advice started, from the man able to get away for ten hours every day and have a break from the relentless whining: how to hold him, how to feed him, how to wind him, not to shake him, and in between regularly reminding me that the six weeks of abstinence the midwife recommended had long passed. That was when I bought the costume, when I realized he was thinking about sex while I was thinking about ways to kill myself, when I knew without doubt we had run out of middle ground.

Having Ben changed me into something I had no idea how to be: a mother. I had expected it to come naturally, but for me it didn't. And the fact that parenthood came so easily to Red made it worse. He stepped into the role of father as if his whole life had been leading to it, as if it were the culmination of everything he was and had ever wanted.

Finally, a few days before Ben's first birthday, Red had had enough. He said it was the swimming costume, that it made him feel bad.

Like a rapist.

When I realized his suitcase was already packed, sitting on the floor beside the door, that he was not raising the issue as an agenda item up for discussion, that what he was actually doing was informing me of the decision he had already made, I tensed, the anger coiled up inside me as tight as in a cat psyching up to the pounce.

Then he picked up Ben.

If a proper mother should have argued, should have insisted that the offspring remain with her, I was not a proper mother. My experience was that motherhood was a façade, a fabrication that sometimes took sixteen years to unravel, but occasionally just the one single year was adequate. I held the front door wide for them both to leave and I felt two things. The first was disappointment. About all the time I had invested, all that energy wasted. As a woman, both as a mother and a partner, I had failed. The second feeling was sadness, sadness and disbelief, that a single elastic garment could be held to blame:

Exhibit one, your honour!

As if that one tiny item had ever been large enough to bear responsibility for everything.

From downstairs I heard laughter. I stood up and got started. I plumped and straightened the bed, wiped down the window ledge, moved Ben's car to the passage outside the room, then swept the floor and mopped it. Finished, I could see no point returning the car to the same spot it had occupied for years like a memorial, so I picked it up, carried it downstairs and left it by the front door.

They were watching TV when I went back into the living room, on the settee together, with Lemon's arm around Ben's shoulders and Ben's head virtually wedged up into Lemon's armpit, watching one of those patronizing children's programmes where there was a huge focus on covering guests with snot-like goo, and the presenters shouted every word they spoke and leapt about like they were high on E. The kind of senseless show I detested, and they were laughing their heads off. Both of them. As though it was the funniest thing either had seen in some time. And they were oblivious to my presence. They noticed me twice; once when I swept the floor in front of the TV, and the second time when I mopped the same spot.

Ben was in his element. Normally I never allowed him to watch stuff like that, but that day, everything was out of control. Berris was out. Lemon was here. The cinema had been a disaster and now my home was filled with a cacophony of screams from the TV and its audience of two, locked into each other's arms like old mates. Finished, I sat down at the table pretending to read and, at some point, Ben stood up

43

to go to the toilet. On his return he spoke to me for the first time since lunch.

'Why's my car in the passage?'

'I'm throwing it out. It's too small for you. That's why.'

'But that's my favourite car.'

'Really? When's the last time you played with it?'

'But it's mine. I don't want you to throw it away.'

'Look, I don't want to have a full-blown discussion about it. You don't play with it any more and it's too small for you even if you did want to. It's pointless keeping it. It's going in the bin.'

He was silent for a moment. He glanced over at Lemon, probably hoping for some support from that quarter. When none was forthcoming he looked down at the floor. 'I wish you was dead,' he said, his voice so low I thought I had misheard.

'What did you say?'

He looked up at me, eyes full of tears. 'I wish you was dead!' he shouted. 'I hate you I hate you I hate you I hate you I hate you!' and fell upon me, kicking and punching and biting and scratching and wailing at the top of his voice, deranged and hysterical.

For a moment, I was completely immobilized. He could have said anything else in the world to me and it might have been okay. But those words were too terrible. What had I ever done to him that was bad enough for him to wish that? I pulled him away from me with one hand and with the other I slapped him hard across the face. There was a moment of shocked silence, a deep sucking in of breath on Ben's part and then he let loose one mighty piece of screaming.

Lemon jumped up from the settee and ran over to him, picking him up and cuddling him. Ben locked his arms around Lemon's neck and his legs tight around his waist. He threw back his head and howled at the top of his lungs.

I too was stunned. It could only have been a few seconds that I stood there, mouth open, to say what, I have no idea, but at some point I realized the phone was ringing. On automatic pilot I walked over and picked up the handset from on top of the TV.

'Hello?' I said. Over Ben's screams it was impossible to hear what was being said. I put my free hand over the other ear, listening hard.

'... see if he's okay...Look, what the fuck is going on over there?'

It was Red.

Thirty minutes later he arrived and took Ben from Lemon without a word. The moment Ben saw Red the sniffs grew worse and as soon as he was in his dad's arms he began to cry again, letting loose the proportion of distress he had deliberately held back for the moment of his grand finale.

Cuddling and kissing Ben as though he too was close to breaking down, Red took him out to the car, where he mollified him for another five minutes before returning to collect his bag.

He was as angry as I had ever seen him. An involuntary tick pulsed at the edge of his left eye. He picked up Ben's bag, then turned to face Lemon, who stood beside me.

'Do you mind?' he asked.

'Sorry,' Lemon said, but instead of leaving the room, he went and sat down on the settee, as if he was suddenly fully engaged in watching the TV and by some miracle was giving us the privacy Red had been too subtle requesting.

'I know how it looks,' I said, 'but Ben...'

Red's hand came up in a Stop sign. 'Just don't! Don't you dare blame him.'

'I wasn't going to *blame* him...'

'I don't wanna hear it,' he said. 'This is the end of the line. I'm not doing this any more.'

'If you would just let me explain...'

'But I don't care what your reasons are. He's been here for five hours. You haven't seen him for a fortnight. How could things get this bad so quick?'

'Red, if you would just listen...'

'But it's just more rubbish. He's a little boy. Four years old! Don't you think he's already got enough on his plate?'

I didn't answer, because what was on his plate was me: absent mum, useless mum, bad mum. I knew it and I didn't want to discuss it in more detail in front of Lemon, but Red was on a roll.

'You don't visit. You don't phone. You don't do anything. *I'm* the one going round mopping up, making good, lying to him so he thinks, despite everything you do and every word you say, that you care. Well, I'm done with it. No more.'

All I wanted to do was wrap the discussion up as quickly as possible. 'It's obvious there's no point trying to discuss this with you, so where do we go from here?' I asked.

'I'm not bringing him any more. You want to see him, you come to *our* home and see him there. You wanna talk to him, pick up the phone and ring.' He glanced at Lemon lounging on the settee in his dressing gown, like a sugar daddy. 'Assuming you can make the time.'

'You seem to have forgotten something; he's my son too!'

'Really?' Red asked, looking at me, waiting for more, but I could see no need to elaborate. The fact that I was Ben's mother was irrrefutable. He shifted the bag to his other hand and turned around to leave. He was almost through the living-room door when he stopped and turned around. The anger was gone, replaced by an expression I could not identify.

'Do you know he cries for you?' he asked. 'Did you know that?'

He watched me for a moment, waiting for a response, but it was so inconceivable I could think of nothing to say. Then he waved his hand as if I were a waste of space, dismissing me. He left the room and a moment later the front door slammed shut.

And then, in case the whole thing wasn't already bloody obvious, and only Lemon had been endowed with sufficient insight to recognize this was not a positive development, at that moment he turned around to look at me, shook his head slowly and said, 'Hope you don't think I'm minding you business when I say that did not go well at all, at all, at all.'

3

Although it was not yet three, and early in the day even by my standards, I poured myself a glass of wine. I did not offer Lemon a drink. The rational part of me knew that the episode with Red and Ben was not Lemon's fault, but another part of me held everything that had happened firmly against him; if it had not been for him I would have changed my clothes and gone to the park instead of the cinema, so there would have been no wet trousers and no scene. If he had not been here when we returned, Ben would have been paying attention to *me* and because I would have been paying attention *back* there would have been no cleaning done upstairs and the old car would still be sitting in the corner of the bedroom gathering dust. If it had not been for him, my head wouldn't have been so filled with Berris that I could hardly think properly, never mind function. No matter which angle I approached from, Lemon sat squarely in the way, and however much I tried, it was impossible to push the blame beyond him.

He helped himself to a vodka on the rocks anyway, watching me all the while, giving me a look that asked: *Well? Are we going to talk about this or not?* It was a look I pretended not to understand; my private business was nothing to do with him. Instead, I fixed my face into an A*sk me any questions and I'll chop your head off* look to keep him at bay. And so for a while he said nothing.

He looked comfortable leaning on the counter, glass raised, examining the contents as though it were the first time he'd ever had the opportunity to study the clarity of vodka at leisure. It wound me up that he dared to look relaxed when my life was breaking down around me. Then I realized that whatever he did would wind me up because it wasn't the things he did that pissed me off so badly, it was *him*. Why had I asked him to stay? I had succumbed to a moment of weakness, a desire to confess the unspeakable, had believed that somehow this man could deliver me, as if such a thing was possible, as if life had not already taught me that the only person I could ever truly depend on was me, and I felt as angry with myself as I did with him, that I had been stupid enough to believe that anything good could ever come from bringing history into my home. It was as much my fault as it was his, and not talking to him was childish and ridiculous. This knowledge, though obvious, instead of making me behave differently however, simply increased my resentment.

I carried my drink into the living room and he followed. I sat on the settee and he sat down beside me. I shifted over a bit towards the end, so we were further apart. He reached over and switched the telly off. When he turned around to face me, I could tell from his expression he intended to stall no longer and I began gathering a few openly hostile responses in my mind to bring to any discussion concerning me or anything I considered to be My Business.

'You know I'va son, don't you?' he said.

'Yes,' I answered.

'You know how long I never see him?'

'Nope.'

'Guess.'

'I'm not really in the mood for guessing games...'

'Thirty-two years,' he said. 'From the day me and Mavis came to England till the day I took her back home to get bury. Left him behind with Mavis' sister, the oldest one. She was still living with Mavis' mum. There was plenty space for the boy to run round, 'nough people to watch over him. Was only supposed to be for a year or two, now here we are.'

He sighed, as though he had finished talking. I waited for what felt like a long while before saying, 'I'm assuming there is actually going to be more, that you were actually endeavouring to make a point?'

'I wrote to him, after Mavis pass,' he said, his tone neutral, as though he hadn't heard me speak and was continuing of his own accord. 'First letter I ever write him. Mavis used to write all the time, think sometimes two, three letters a month. We never had no more kids after we come here, and well, I wasn't around much, working working working, come night-time out with me friends, as you know. Think she was probably bored most the time. And lonely. But she never said a word. Never said, "'Isn't it 'bout time you start stay in?" or nothing. Can't remember her complaining about a thing, all the years we was married, 'cept the cold of course, always the cold. Never could get used to it, no matter how long we live here. Couldn't stand it at all. Anyway.

'Though I was never one for writing and such like, I wrote him when she died. He moved to the States 'bout ten years ago. New York. Married an American woman out there. You might think it strange I never just ring but after all the years I never ring when she was alive, was a habit hard to suddenly break after she pass. So I wrote him, told him 'bout the funeral arrangements, etcetera. Mavis always say she never wanted to be bury here in the cold ground for all eternity, so I took her back home, like she wanted. Wrote and tell the boy the date and time. He came over on the day. Never brung the wife but he came – thirty-two years I never seen him till then – and he brung the grandkids.'

He put down his glass and ran his palms over his trousers as though trying to smooth out any creases. I had seen people do this in the undertakers, occupying their hands as if doing so straightened out the thoughts in their minds and made it possible for them to say things they could not otherwise say. I remembered an elderly Jamaican woman, widowed two days, who stood beside her husband's casket twisting her handkerchief between her hands for half an hour, then saying, 'I'll never forgive him for this.' I looked down at the floor and Lemon carried on.

'Course I knew they was born, Mavis tell me and I seen the pictures John send, but at the funeral was the first time

I actually laid eyes on them in the flesh. Two boys and a girl. The girl...'

He was grappling for words though I didn't know why. He was a natural storyteller and, angry as I was with him, I was entranced.

'At the graveside, I was crying, man, couldn't stop. Anyway, I felt something and I look down and she was holding my hand real tight, and she smile at me. You know, if Mavis wasn't six foot under by then, that's exactly what she woulda done, hold my hand and smile. No words, nothing extra, just a little simple something for me to know she was supporting me, standing by me, like she always done, even all them years when I give her no reason for it, never give her nothing back, but she done it anyway. Now I'm not a man to go with all the jumbie business – though me nah say a word against Jack Lantern, you understand – but I when I look into the girl's eyes, was like looking into her grandma eyes for true and the thing shock me.

'That night, couldn't sleep, just up pacing this way and that till after dawn when there wasn't any point trying to catch sleep again. And I wondered, how could a little nine-year-old girl know to do that, that that was the best thing she coulda done, that nothing else in this life coulda comfort me more? Just a hand. One tiny hand. How could she know? S'impossible, innit?

'I never felt so shame. Every time I think 'bout it, water come to me eye. To know she live nine long years and not once I ever did a thing for her, not a biscuit, not a ginnip, not a bean, and she still give me her hand. Man, it make me feel small.

'John never stop in Montserrat. Went back to the States same night. Had some urgent business to attend – or so him say – so off he went. Didn't get a chance to speak to him or nothing.

'Anyway, I wrote him. Asked after the family and such like, then ask why he don't come up to London. Said I would pay the fare and they just come up and stay by me for a few weeks. He wrote back real polite, not angry or nothing, say he long find comfort in the Church and he have all the father he need right thereso. And you know what? The worse thing of all? I couldn't even say nothing, because the man was right. His whole life I never put myself out even the once. Why should he raise a finger to do something for me now?'

The tale was done, his point made and I bristled.

'Look, no offence right, it's nice of you to share this with me, but my situation is not the same as yours.'

'I never said it was.'

'But that's your point, isn't it? You've messed up with your son, I should try not to mess up with mine.'

'All I'm saying is sometimes you know things need sorting but you don't do it. Someday you might find you dallied so long, the time's passed and you don't have the choice no more.'

'But I've been there for Ben. I've bought him birthday and Christmas presents, and every Easter I get him an egg…'

'And tomorrow?' he asked.

I knew he wasn't asking about the one day, he meant the future; tomorrow and the day after and all the tomorrows thereafter, but I responded literally.

'Tomorrow, I'll go and take some advice. In law, Red doesn't have a leg to stand on. He can't stop me seeing my son. It's my legal right.'

'You legal right,' he repeated slowly, like he was feeling the words in his mouth, exploring them, rolling them around. As though he had been talking about rum and I had brought up rhubarb. When he looked at me, his eyes held something in the way of contempt.

'I need some decent food,' he said. 'I'm gonna go do some shopping and when I get back, I'll cook.'

'Fine. Whatever.'

'I take it when I get back you gonna let me in?' he said.

He was offering me a choice. When I looked at him his eyes were speaking again, mocking me: *I know you*, they said, *know the type very well. You're a runner. A duck-and-diver. Scared.*

'You can take my key,' I said, getting up. 'That should reduce some of your worry, shouldn't it?'

Having given him the key so he could go shopping to buy the things he needed to cook, I naturally expected him to have the money to pay for them, but he did not. When he asked me for money, I collected my purse, grudgingly pulled out a couple of twenty-pound notes, and handed them over without meeting his eyes.

I gave him a curt nod on his return home. He was laden with so many carrier bags it looked like he had done the whole week's shopping. Though I wondered when I saw the mass of food he had bought, I could not quite bring myself to open my mouth and enquire just exactly how long he planned on staying. Nor to mention, though it hadn't escaped my notice, that he hadn't had the courtesy to hand back any change.

It was not my intention to make him feel self-conscious – it would have been pointless anyway; the man was immune to subtlety – but I sat on the high stool in front of the breakfast bar scowling as he hummed and unloaded some of the bags, then began searching the entire pot cupboard for a suitable vessel in which to bubble up his concoction.

As soon as he had hoisted the pumpkin out from inside one of the bags, a piece that was about a quarter of the size of a large one, burnt-orange flesh oozing moist white pips, I knew what he was making. What else would a Montserratian man shop for and cook on a Saturday? It was such a stereotype that on another day, in better humour, I might have chuckled. He was making soup.

I watched as he exerted himself, thwacking the skin off the pumpkin, reducing the flesh to fine-slivered squares, then chopping the cucumber and onions while the kettle boiled. Everything went into the pot on the stove and he lit the fire beneath it.

My mother had cooked pumpkin soup on Saturdays, virtually every Saturday when I was young, yet I had forgotten. Somehow, it had slipped my mind. Lemon had eaten here, eaten *that* here, years back, laughing and blowing hot spoonfuls with Berris. He was contriving to look innocent, but I damn well knew the only reason he was cooking soup now was to take me back to then.

Without asking he turned on the kitchen radio. It was set to Classic FM. Bach's *Magnificat* ceased abruptly as Lemon began to retune the station, turning the volume up in an effort to hear the faintest illegal transmissions of reggae pirate-radio stations, and the static crackling and hissing, the tuning in and out of stations he had no interest in, went on at length, stretching my poor nerves till I felt like a passenger travelling on a fast train beside an open window.

He found a station of his choice finally, an old-style giggip-giggip channel, playing the weary, slow reggae of singers long dead. To raise them, he whacked the volume up as high as it could go.

My eyes followed him back to the sink where he washed the lamb, lifting the pieces out, and trimmed off the fat and bloodied edges with fingers that went about their task deftly. Compared with how clumsy his handling was of the table knife I gave him last night with dinner, he wielded the meat cleaver with the finesse of a pro.

All the while, he kept a lit cigarette poised in the right-hand side of his mouth. He kept the smoke out of his eyes by keeping the right eye half closed and his head tilted slightly to the left.

I watched.

He put the lamb into the pot and emptied another kettle-ful of hot water over it. He selected a few choice branches of thyme, ran the water over them at the sink, shook the excess off as though he were shaking down the mercury in a thermometer, then tossed them into the cauldron as well. He rummaged in the cutlery drawer for a ladle, positioned himself in front of the cooker and, with his back to me, as uninhibited as if I was not sitting there watching him and scowling at all, as he stirred the pot, he started to dance.

Instantly, the room was filled with the aroma of soup beginnings, the earliest stage when all the ingredients still retained their own fresh and heightened smells, an aroma that was a group or sequence of different scents that assailed individually, till the fragrant thyme finally rose to dominate. Then, on the back of the record before it, from the radio came the instrumental sounds of 'Mr Bojangles', and John Holt's smooth vocals began to croon about the very first time he'd met him.

There were things I no longer believed in. God was one; a pretty straightforward process of elimination had clarified that issue once my mother was dead. And all the stuff she believed in, that they all believed in, their generation, the spirits and jumbies and obeah, the miscellaneous hocus pocus, all of that nonsense I had thrown out years ago. I was not a spiritual person. I did not believe in karma – of which I had seen little evidence – or fate or destiny or anything along those lines. It goes without saying that listening to someone explain an out-of-body experience would have produced little more response from me than a sneer.

Yet I don't know how else to describe it. The combination of the soup and the music and Lemon throwing down moves like he was Mr Bojangles himself, and I had a feeling, like déjà vu, as if the whole universe and every sound and atom of air inside it had curved sharply and was blasted back on rewind at warp speed, and suddenly the kitchen was full of glamorous bejewelled women, and sharply dressed men, the air filled with the smell of party foods: lamb curry, rice and peas, beef patties, goat water, salt-fish fritters and fried chicken. There were drinks galore, the hard stuff, rum and vodka and whisky and brandy, and everyone had a glass, drinking and chatting away in voices that sounded like they were cussing each other, drowned out by loud and regular laughter.

Over in the corner stood Berris on his own, sucking on a toothpick, immaculately dressed even by his standards, dripping gold from every part of his body that could sustain it, sipping whisky chased with water, red-eyed from the marijuana he had been smoking, green-eyed with petty rage, staring through the open double doors between the kitchen and the living room.

In the living room, calypso blared, Arrow's 'Hot Hot Hot', and a sea of bodies bobbed and swayed, arms raised, backs bending, hips bumping, waists winding, and in the midst of them all, my mother, the best dancer of all the women there, and Lemon, the best man, bouncing off each other's bodies in a perfect passion of rhythm and style.

Finally, Berris put his drink down on the counter closest to him and removed the toothpick from his lips. He dropped it into the glass and began making his way towards them. His gait was brisk and sure, like a bulldog on muscular legs slightly bowed, his shoulders moving as if they too were strolling, left right left right left. In his expression there was no trace of anger or malice. Instead his features were set hard into the focused expression of a man who had repulsive but necessary tasks to perform; the man responsible for garbage disposal or sewage clearance, the person charged with vermin exterminations.

Only his eyes blazed.

All but two of the people in the house that night were aware of him as he walked, and the wave of bodies across his path parted as if he were Moses himself. For a man who danced badly, there was grace in the fluid swing of his arm, and my mother spun across the room in a clumsy pirouette for one who danced so well. She landed on the floor in shock and it was only after she touched her nose and saw blood that she even realized what had happened. By then, Berris had passed her en route to the record player. There he dragged up the stylus in a loud and permanent scrape across the LP. In the quiet, no one spoke. Berris looked around, like a proud father at his daughter's wedding, just checking he had everyone's attention, about to commence his speech: *ting ting ting*. It must have been a trick of the dark, but he appeared taller, his chest fuller. He had but the two words to say to the people watching, and when he spoke his voice was loud but calm.

'Party done.'

When I came to I was lying on the settee. I felt dizzy and confused. There was a pillow under my head and a blanket over my body. It was dark outside and the living-room lights were on. Kneeling on the floor beside the settee was Lemon, his hand on my forehead, like he was checking to see if I had a temperature. There was a pain towards the back of my head, above the left ear, like I had taken a hard blow. I looked around the room, trying to get my bearings. It was the decor that was out of place. My mind was in the wrong era. She was not here and had not been for years.

'What happened?' I asked. My throat was dry and I cleared it.

Using his thumb, he pulled back my eyelids, first one then the other, examining my pupils, looking for signs of concussion I guessed.

'You passed out. But not to worry. I gotta strong feeling you gonna live.'

'Super,' I said.

I tried to sit up, but the effort required was too much. I flopped back down and Lemon adjusted the blanket gently.

'You have somewhere to go?' he asked.

'No.'

'Then rest up. Relax. S'about time you start take care of youself.'

I thought about my life, tried to think of a single good thing in it, just the smallest reason to want to live, to care enough either way, and found nothing.

'Why?' I asked. 'What's the point?'

'What no kill you make you strong.'

'Spare me the cheery sermons, please.'

He looked at me like I imagined I looked at Ben sometimes. As though I was a difficult child and he was doing his best to not rise to it. He picked up a bowl containing water and a flannel from where he had placed it on the floor beside him and I realized while I had been unconscious he had obviously been using it to wipe my head. It felt like the greatest act of kindness anyone had done for me in years, that simple functional task: dipping, squeezing, dabbing. To my horror I felt tears prickling the surface of my eyes.

'I'd really prefer to be left alone,' I said.

He stood up. 'Let me get you some soup.'

Oohh, that soup, that soup, that soup; it was heaven. Not too runny, not too thick, the consistency was perfect. Saffron-coloured and bursting with flavour, with small, soft pieces of yam and sweet potato and green banana and tania seed, and chewy torpedo dumplings. The lamb was not overcooked till it fell from the bone, but had retained its elasticity. Every mouthful bore deliciously delicate treats: carrots and pearl barley and christophine and lima beans. He sat beside me on the settee and fed me like he must have done his wife, slow, careful, spoonful by spoonful. I recalled the story of Rapunzel and her barren, unhappy mother who, having tasted the salad pilfered from the witch's garden, decided she must have more of it or die. With every swallow, how I identified with her.

And as I ate in wonder, Lemon spoke non-stop, voice low, as if I were too infirm to converse back and it was incumbent on him to keep the conversation going single-handed. The most important ingredient was the pumpkin. Once the pumpkin was good, you were halfway there. And you had to know the difference between what you wanted boiled into the soup for flavour and what should be kept back and added later. And you needed to know when the lamb was cooked, the point at which it should be removed from the pot, to be later returned. Timing was everything. To cook a perfect pot of soup, you had first to learn how to tell the time.

When the contents of the bowl had been polished off, I offered up the three words that best expressed my feelings.

'I want more,' I said.

He looked at me and smiled. It was the first time he had smiled since his arrival. I had forgotten how charming it was, how attractive it made him. He had one of those smiles that engaged every feature on his face, his wide mouth, his lean cheeks, his eyes, the creased skin at their corners. When he smiled at you it was as if you had his fullest attention; no one else existed for him anywhere. It was irresistible. I felt myself smiling back as he rose and left to bring me seconds.

I felt different. In the centre of my feelings, like the eye of a tornado, the anger held its ground, but around the edges I could feel it giving way to something softer that made me feel uncomfortable. Vulnerable. I wished I had the capacity to just enjoy the moment, to embrace the pleasure of having things done for me, but it was not in me. Instead, I found myself wondering what was in it for him, why he was doing this, and just how bad the sting would be that brought me back down to earth.

When he returned I was happy to see the bowl was almost as full as it had been last time. Carefully he settled on the floor beside the settee, moving slowly, careful not to spill a drop. I reached out and took the bowl from him, turning to lie on my side so I could feed myself.

'You sure you can manage?' he asked.

'Yes. Why are you doing this?'

'Got nothing else to do.'

'That's not a good enough answer.'

'It's the best answer you gonna get.'

'I don't want the "best answer", I want the truth.' I waited, but he didn't reply. 'You visited him, didn't you, in prison? That's why he came to see you.'

He shook his head. 'Me and Berris go back a ways. We had unfinished business, things that needed to be said.'

'About my mother?'

He shrugged. 'And other things.'

'Like?'

'You asking me to number and reel them off? Most stories are like that bowl of soup you eating now, a whole heap of ingredients put together at the proper time. You can't pick up one thing on its own, piece of dasheen say, and study it then walk and tell people you gotta understanding of soup. You have to start with the things that need to go in the pot first. You want the truth, I gotta start at the beginning.'

'So start at the beginning then,' I said, wondering where the beginning of my own confession lay. Not the night of the engagement party, *ting ting ting*. By then things were already in full swing. The beginning was back further. Months back.

'Now?' he asked.

'Yes now.'

'I need a drink.'

'So? Get one.'

He was slow to stand, unsure but going along with it. He rubbed his hands together, psyching himself up.

'You want one as well?'

'Sure,' I answered. 'Why not?'

*

'We growed up together, me and Berris both. In Cudjoe Head. North Montserrat. People say his father never want to know him from when he born. Don't know if it's true but it don't matter anyhow, 'cos Berris believe it to be so.

'His mother put him to board with Mistress Jolly when she went to Curaçao. Visited a few times but never come back to get him or send ticket for him to come. Wasn't no work in Montserrat then. Yeah, there was the odd cleaning job in one of the hotel or rich people house, but you couldn't live off what you earn there. Folks had to go to the other islands. At that time was mostly Curaçao they went. Had sugar and coffee and oil there. Was work to be had, and money.

'They went off. Send back whatever they could to keep the kids. Pretty sure his mum done that, same as everybody else, but Berris say if she did, he never see a cent. Mistress Jolly tell him his mother never send a bean. Type of person she was, can't see she woulda keep him for nothing. But that's what she say and that's what the man believe.

'We was raggedy. All the kids was raggedy then. Had but the two pair of trouser, one for church and one for school. You never wear you church trouser to school 'less you want you arse cut, and you school pants you take off soon as you reach home in case you wear those out before time and have to go school with you arse outta door. Must be only a handful had shoes and them what did was lucky if they fit. I remember Orlando Weekes, schoolteacher son. Boy used to bawl fire because the shoes be biting him all day and his mother make him keep them on. Boy used to limp like a dog with a crab on him paw. Girl, we were raggedy then. Raggedy. Times was rough and all of us together was poor.

'But it come like Berris was worse off. Don't know if it was the hair or what. We used to go down by Mas' Cook. Mas' Cook was a handicap. Had short legs but might as wella had no legs and done 'cos they never work. Used to pull hisself 'long on him backside with the hands. Come like after a while you hardly even notice 'cos he move so fast. He's the one person I know them times make a good living. Man used to make mat and basket from reed and they was always by the gate for people to see and buy. And he used to cut hair. He cut all our hair. Would chap you in the head if you move once he start cut. Most times you get a skiffle you hadda lump on you head you never start out with.

'But Berris never have his hair cut. Or even plait. Used to look nasty. Kids being kids they take the piss outta him bad. Must be that why he learn to fight so hard. Got so no one tease him any more 'cos when he fight you, it's like say he wanna kill you, even the girls...'specially the girls. Always had to be someone there to stop him, 'cos from when we was boys till we come men, I never once seen him stop hisself.

'All of us was living with family, the grandparents, or an auntie or some such. I live with my father's sister then, and girl let me tell you that woman was a devil. But she was nothing next to Mistress Jolly. Berris' mum family never want no truck with her bastard pickney, so she *had* to leave him with Mistress Jolly, never had no choice the way I see it, though to hear Berris talk you'd swear she had 'nough. Mistress Jolly take in a whole heapa kids, 'nough jingbang, collect a whole heapa money, but she keep near 'nough every dollar for sheself.

'That woman was always vex for something. You might as well say "switch live in her hand", 'cos it was there from sunrise till sunfall. Only time she put it by was Sunday morning when she go church and odd time the parents come. Barring that, them kids get some licks you see. 'Nough licks, man, 'nough licks.

'None of us had much food then. Was mostly vegetarian but not from choice. If there was piece a meat in you house and you lucky, you peas might catch little the flavour, but the only time you had a solid chance of meat on you plate was Christmas Day and Easter, and even then was no guarantee.

'Mistress Jolly was always walking and talking 'bout how the orphans was eating her out of house and home, but they must have been some serious slow eaters, 'cos the house was always being fix: new roof, extension, big old comfy chair. And that woman was fat! She was fat till fat roll when she walk. To look at her you would never say she was someone who live far from the kitchen.

'But Berris was small. All Mistress Jolly pickney was small. We never have much but I still save a dumpling for Berris from my soup, or little dasheen, small piece of yam. Up to now don't know why. 'Cept I seen him cry. Something pitiful. When he thought was no one there to see, I saw. See him put down some piece of bawling, never seen nothing like it in my life. Guess I felt sorry for him or something. Anyways I did it, give him a little food regular like. According to him was that little something save his life. Think that's how we growed up to be so close.'

He paused for a moment and lit a cigarette. With a grimace, he swallowed a mouthful from his glass, then took a deep drag and exhaled.

'He call me a fool when I marry Mavis.' His voice was quieter now, tired. 'Think that was the only time we nearly come to blows. Said she was easy, I wasn't the first to fuck her, that she take me and make jacket to give her bastard a name. She never forget that. Never forgived him neither. After we come to England I still use to see him, we was still tight, but he couldn't visit my yard. Was his fault for true and probably serve him right, but he still hate her for it. Hate her bad.

'Course Mavis tell me all was lie, Berris jealous, the kinda thing she *had* to say, if you think on it, and I listen to what she have to say, but I study my son when he born, study him hard to see what he have for me. Like you, he favour his mum bad. Never could see me in him 't'all. Think that was the reason I never send for him, even when we get settle here and we coulda.

'Deep down in my heart, all that time, I never knowed, never knowed for sure...was he mine?'

'Are you telling me all those years you never had a relationship with your son was 'cos of what Berris said?' I asked.

The soup was finished. I replaced the spoon in the bowl as he took it, nodding. 'Yep.'

'So he said one thing and your wife said something completely different and, of the two, you believed *him*?'

'You wanted the truth, that's what you getting.'

'Just so I'm clear, *you* messed up but it was Berris's fault?'

'I'm not making excuses…'

'Yes you are! So what that he said it? So what?'

'I did what I did. Can't turn back the clock. All I'm trying to do is tell it like it was,' he said.

He raised his brows, his hands, his shoulders in a shrug, and all at once he looked old. How many lives had Berris trashed in his lifetime, I wondered? How many? And yet Lemon still stood by him, still visited, still had him round for talks on old times. Even though I felt like a bully, like I was beating someone up who was making no effort to defend himself, I couldn't stop.

'She was your wife.' To my surprise, my voice was choked. 'Why couldn't you just believe her?'

'You think I didn't want to believe her? You think I never try? Girl, you can't even begin to imagine my misery, the ways I let her down. What I told you ain't nothing.'

'What, there's more?'

'Always more. But I need to get a refill first. You want one?'

I shook my head. I had been concentrating on eating. The glass of wine he'd brought me was still full.

'Think I better have some soup first; line me stomach a bit.'

'Okay,' I said, and he went.

There was a time when I would have been overjoyed to know just how dissipated Lemon's family life was. Clearly, since then, I had grown up. Now I just felt angry with Lemon, angry he had given Berris free reign to manipulate his thoughts, then done little else other than sit back and accept the resulting unhappiness, like a willing victim patiently poised, awaiting a fatal stab in the back.

I asked him why he had come to see me and he had started from the beginning, with his childhood, and Berris was there. Berris was at my own beginning too. Everything had begun with him, literally begun from the first moment I laid eyes on him here in this very house. Up until then, my childhood had been spectacularly humdrum. It had chugged along with the monotony of a fairy tale; the odd discomfort here and there swiftly resolved and resulting in a happy-ever-after. It had been solid, unwavering and predictable. Like my friendship with Sam, my best friend from the day I started secondary school and found myself in the formroom sitting beside her. Samantha Adebayo. She was also at the beginning. My life changed on a day that started with Sam, the day we counted virgins and netball practice got cancelled.

Considering it was the moment that signalled the beginning of the end of my childhood, you might have thought something dramatic had marked it out; a blazing comet crossing the sky or thunder pounding like a roll of drums. Instead it was a usual day, completely normal, a day so ordinary that I hadn't suspected a thing.

4

I waited for Sam on the corner of Amhurst Road and Dalston Lane, outside Easton Chemist's, at the bottom of Pembury Estate where she lived with her family, the whole of the Adebayo posse; her mum and dad, herself and three younger brothers.

Her family was the complete opposite of mine, where it was just me and my mum and everything was quiet and in its place. Her dad was kind of okay but Mrs Adebayo could be a bit weird. Because of her, I didn't visit them much, but on the occasions I had, Sam's house was as noisy and crazy and manic as the school dining hall at lunchtime. Compared to hers, my house was like a morgue.

From where I stood I could see through the courtyard, almost to the middle of the estate. The Adebayos lived in the block right at the top, overlooking the park, and there were several exits between that end and where I stood, but I knew Sam would come out this way because she always did. This was where I met her every morning; a short walk down from where I lived and across the road from Hackney Downs Station where we caught the 48 bus to take us to school.

I was digi because it was a Monday and on Mondays after school we had netball practice. About half the time, Sam forgot her kit. She was pretty scatty, forever leaving something behind or just forgetting things completely. I was digi because I didn't want to end up at practice on my own. But the minute I saw her, I relaxed.

She was running from the moment she came into view, racing through the estate in the disgusting maroon uniform we hated so much, satchel flapping, blazer and cardigan undone, the carrier bag with her kit in it held between her teeth, her hands busy pulling her auburn hair into a ponytail; late as usual and still not finished dressing.

'Jay, you gotta stop letting your mum do your hair, man,' she said as she reached me, slowing down to a walk, which I picked up alongside her. My mum had washed my hair the day before and spent the evening cornrowing it into fine plaits that ran from my forehead to the nape of my neck, like Leroy's from *Fame*.

'I'll take them out for you at first break,' she said.

Up until then, I'd quite liked the style, but if Sam thought it was dry, it would have to go.

'Okay.'

'You done your biology?' she asked.

I nodded.

'Man, I can't do shit at home. You don't know how lucky you are. Once I've finished my O levels I'm out of there. My family's seriously fucked.'

71

We were five months away from our O levels and the end of our school days for ever. It was kind of strange knowing that, like the end of school was supposed to mark the beginning of being grown up, but I didn't feel grown up at all. I didn't have the first idea about what I wanted to do with my life. The only thing I was good at was writing stories, but that wasn't much use when you were trying to work out what kind of career you could end up with. That was another difference between me and Sam. She always knew exactly what she wanted to do and no matter what, she went ahead and did it. Her mother was English and her father Ghanaian and she was totally against mixed relationships. She was sick of her parents arguing all the time, sick of being in a two-bedroomed flat and not having her own bedroom, sick of being the only girl in her family and having to slave behind her brothers, and sick of being told what to do. As soon as our exams were over, she was leaving home.

'You should've come over the garages on Friday,' she said.

She was talking about the car park underneath the tower blocks on Nightingale Estate. There were always loads of guys hanging out from the estate down there, renters mostly, trying to get the girls who passed through into the empty garages on a one-to-one. I didn't like the scene as much as she did and it wasn't just because the boys all seemed so immature, or even because the second they laid eyes on Sam it was like I'd suddenly become invisible. I had a deeper personal problem: French kissing. I'd never done it. You couldn't count the hours spent practising on oranges; cutting them in half and gouging out the fruit using only my tongue.

Good French-kissers left the pith clean, but I was nowhere near that level of proficiency. Usually, I just ended up with an exhausted tongue, and sore bits at the corners of my mouth so that when the juice touched them it stung like hell. I was terrified my inexperience would make me look ridiculous, and over the garages, that fear made me mute.

'Was it good?'

'It was wicked. I got asked out again.'

'Who by?'

'Donovan, innit! Jay, if I tell you something, you gotta promise me you'll never tell anyone as long as you live.'

She was so dramatic. 'Like *I'd* tell anyone,' I said, rolling my eyes.

'You have to promise me. Swear on your mother's life.'

'I swear, okay?'

'I saw his wood.'

'Liar!' I shrieked.

'I swear.'

'I don't believe you.'

'You think I'd lie about something like that?'

'How did you see it?'

'He took it out. He wannid me to touch it –'

'Ergh! Gross.'

'But I said "no", of course,' she added, but it sounded kind of lame, like maybe she had only added that last bit because of how I'd reacted, and I wondered whether she really had touched it.

Donovan was in the sixth form at Homerton House. He had been asking her out for months, and the way she told, it was like he was some renter and she just wasn't interested. But I knew she had *some* interest, because I caught them kissing once, one evening when all the kids were playing out on my road and we decided to play Knock Down Ginger with the old fogies who lived on the first floor in Bodney Mansions. But when we took the corner into the dark stairwell, Donovan and Sam were already there, doing some serious kissing and grinding up. She looked well shamed when she saw me, and they both tried to play it like nothing had been going on. But it was blatant. I'd caught them cold.

'So what did it look like?' I asked.

'Like a saveloy when the skin's peeled back.'

'Ugh! I am *never* gonna eat saveloy ever again,' I said.

'When I'm older, I'm only gonna go out with white guys,' Sam said.

'Why?'

'Coloured people are more sexed than white people. That's what my mum says. That's why they shouldn't mix.'

This was news to me and I was quiet as I digested it. Because she had one black and one white parent, Sam was an expert on everything to do with colour. I was lucky to have her as a friend. I learned a lot from her.

The bus stop was crowded with people, including two African boys from Shoreditch School, who were usually at this stop in the mornings. One of them fancied Sam. He tried to pretend he never saw us, but he was just styling it. His friend gave him a butt with his elbow in the stomach, then started to laugh.

'Stupid bubus!' Sam said, loud enough for them to hear. She called all Africans 'bubus', even her dad. Then, turning to me, she whispered, 'Ugh! Can you imagine me and one of those bubus doing The Nasty?'

For an instant, my imagination ran riot. I stared at Sam, she stared at me. There was silence. Then we both cracked up.

I started taking the cornrows out during biology and by first break they were gone.

'I wanted you to look like Farrah but it ain't happening, man,' Sam said, as she teased my hair into large curls that fell out as soon as she let them go. According to her, Farrah Fawcett-Majors wasn't just the best looking of the three Charlie's Angels, she was the most beautiful woman in the world. *She* was the woman who should have played Lois Lane opposite Christopher Reeve, the world's best-looking man.

We were in the girls' toilets. It stunk of wee and cigarettes and the manky smell that was always in the changing room after we'd finished PE. My hair was frizzed from being plaited straight after being washed. The Electrocuted Look. I hated it when it was like this.

'I need a hairband, man,' I said.

'You're telling me? One thing I do know, you can't do Farrah with a bushy Afro.'

She pulled a thick elastic band off her wrist where she always had a stash of them and I took it, pulling my hair back into one, smoothing it down as much as possible.

'You better put some water on that, Kizzy,' she said.

I did that, splashed water on it, without looking at her. Sometimes her comments stung, but it wasn't cool to show it. Kizzy was the daughter of Kunta Kinte, the African slave in *Roots*. Sam pushed her face close to the mirror, examining it.

'Shit, Jay! Look at this,' she said, but I blanked her. 'I think I'm getting a zit. Right on the end of my nose as well. That's just fuckry, man.'

Sam had a permanent patch of scarlet mounds on her forehead. The spots that came up on her were always red. Her skin was very pale, whiter than most of the white people I knew, and she had hazel eyes that were just beautiful, and thick hair that was a kind of auburn now but, in summer, bleached in the sun so she had blonde highlights at the front and around the edges, and it was kink-free, like her mum's.

They were a strange bunch, her and her family. They all had the same mum and dad, yet none of them looked alike. Only one of her brothers looked proper half-caste. The middle one was nearly as black as me and the youngest one was as pale as Sam was, but he had red bushy Negro hair. It was like every child in that family had had their parents' genes put into a Coke bottle, shook up, and then a separate burst of spray had been collected to make each of them. They were as different from each other as a litter of kittens.

'I'm gonna squeeze it,' she said, and she did. A few moments later, the site where the teeny pimple had been was ablaze and swollen, as if someone had boxed her.

'Do you know how you can tell for sure if someone's done The Nasty?'

I shook my head without looking at her and she was quiet for a second, clocking me.

'Look, my whole family's doing my head in. At least you know who you are and where you're coming from. A whole of something, not frigging *half* of nothing. I swear, I'm never gonna marry any boy who ain't coming from where I'm coming and put this shit on my kids...' Her face had gone red, like she was blushing badly. The way she always looked when she was about to cry. The silence was broken by the bell. Break was over. I took one last look at my hair, picked my bag up off the floor, then turned to face her.

'How can you tell?' I asked.

She smiled, blinking quickly, relieved. She linked her arm through mine as she hitched her satchel back up on to her shoulder. Though it was only us in the toilets, she glanced around like there might be crowds hiding in the cubicles, ear-wigging. Her voice was low. She began to explain.

We counted the virgins at lunchtime, not just among the other pupils and the whole of the teachers, but the ones walking around the streets too. We saw an old lady on a Zimmer who was about ninety million years old and still hadn't done It, and I cracked up so bad I actually wet myself a bit.

It was so simple, I couldn't believe I had only just found out how to tell. Virgins walked with their toes pointing inwards and those who had done The Nasty, when they walked, their toes pointed out.

On our way into the chip shop at Haggerston Square we passed a group of seven or eight guys from Shoreditch School acting like they thought they were sweet-boys. We queued for ages and took turns drowning our chips with salt and onion vinegar, then carefully tore the bottom off the chip cone so the warm vinegar, instead of ending up dripping out slowly all over our clothes, could just trickle out the one time and done.

The Shoreditch Massive were still loitering a few shops down and, laughing our heads off, we concocted a plan. We came out of the shop and walked past them with our toes pointing so far outwards, we were waddling like a pair of penguins. When we were far enough away to outrun them, Sam turned around and shouted, 'Renters!' and we legged it.

I felt heady with knowledge, the power to look at total strangers and know for sure what they'd been up to. I even found myself studying my own feet as I walked, and Sam's when she wasn't looking. My feet seemed to naturally point inwards, which made sense. But Sam's didn't. Her feet were more or less parallel with each step and I wondered what exactly that meant.

At home time, we discovered netball practice had been cancelled. Sam wanted to go over to Nightingale Estate and mess around in the garages for a while because her mum wasn't expecting her home for another couple of hours, but I was hungry and couldn't be bothered.

Unlike me though, Sam didn't need the company. Once she'd made up her mind about what she wanted to do, that was it. I said I was gonna go home and she decided to go over the garages on her own.

We'd already spent the remainder of our money, what should have been our bus fare home, on rhubarb and custards and pink bon-bons, so we had no choice on the journey home but to trod. Nightingale Estate was just on the other side of the park from the top of my road, so Sam walked with me to my house. We joked about outside for about ten minutes, then she carried on, and I watched her skipping till she disappeared out of sight round the bend at the top of the road.

I let myself in with the key I wore on a shoelace around my neck, having lost the last three keys my mum had given me. Inside, the house was warm and steamy with rice and peas and the smell of curry recently cooked, which was good. I dropped my bags on the floor inside the passage, opened the door to the sitting room and walked in.

My mum was on the settee with a man I'd never seen before. They were kissing so hard that it was a moment before they even realized I was there. I took in a zillion things in a second. His wet red tongue poking into her open mouth. Her blouse undone. His hand inside it. His flies undone. My mum's hand inside the gaping hole there, moving. Sounds, I think from her, like someone who'd been gagged still trying to speak. And her hair, it looked like she'd been in a fight or something! Of the three of us, I don't know who was the most shocked.

She leapt up and turned around so her back was to me and I could tell she was buttoning up her blouse. The man kind of leaned forward with his arms crossed over each other on his lap, as if that was supposed to make me believe his flies were done up now.

'You're home early!' my mother said over her shoulder, but it wasn't a question she was asking, it was an accusation.

'Netball got cancelled,' I said.

She turned around. Her shirt wasn't tucked in properly and she'd left a button undone, just above the waistband of a short black skirt that I'd only ever seen her in once, at the shop, after she'd tried it on. She'd asked me what I thought and we agreed it was too short to wear on the street. She must have gone back without me and bought it. She hadn't needed to keep it a secret, and the fact that she had, though it was a small thing and silly, made me feel hurt. She smoothed down her hair like that smoothed everything over and said to me, as if it were a perfectly normal occasion and that man had just knocked at the front door, 'There's someone I'd like you to meet. This is Uncle Berris.'

When I looked at him, he was staring down at the floor, but he nodded his head at me in a quick flick, smiling in the foolish way the kids in my class did after they put up their hands to answer a question, got picked, then gave the wrong answer. I looked back at my mother. She was wringing her hands together now and smiling at me in a *whatever you do, don't make a fuss* kind of way. Looking at her made me feel like I'd shrunk, then I realized I hadn't, it was her that had grown. I looked down at her feet. She was wearing red clogs with the highest heels I had ever seen her in. And I tried really hard not to notice but it was just blatant that while her heels were neatly together, her toes were definitely pointing out.

*

'He makes cars, toy ones, for children to play with; makes them out of metal, and he fixes things. He's really good with his hands...' – she laughed then at a joke I did not get. 'He's just so nice...and so good-looking. Go on, admit it,' she said, 'he's good-looking, ain't he?'

He was kind of okay for an old guy. He was tall and looked strong. He was dark though, not as dark as me but nowhere near as light as she was, with broad features so sharply shaped it was as if his head had been chiselled out of a smooth piece of dark wood. His hair was skiffled low with a side parting etched on the left-hand side of his scalp, and he had a neat beard that joined his sideburns so that his whole face looked like it was in a black velvet frame. But he was no Superman. And for all his good looks, there was something I didn't like about him, something in the slant of his eyes and his way of not really looking straight at you, but snatching glances instead, which was what he'd done as he was leaving.

Almost as soon as I thought this, I wondered if I was being fair. The fact was I wasn't happy, but I did not know if I was unhappy with him. I really couldn't say what exactly it was that I was unhappy about. All I could think about was what they'd been up to and how many times he'd been here behind my back. And above all of that, I couldn't stop thinking about the position of her toes. Reluctantly, I nodded.

'I'm so glad you like him,' she said, even though I never said that. 'Jinxy, I think I'm in love. I never thought it would happen again. I never thought anyone would make me feel like this...' She laughed again, closing her eyes slowly, smiling like she was remembering something wonderful that had nothing to do with me and I wondered if it was to do with what they were doing inside each other's clothing, her and that man.

'Why did you say he was my uncle?' I asked.

She waved away my small and insignificant point. 'He's a big man and you're a child.'

'I'm not a kid, I'm sixteen. And we're not related.'

'I know that, but you should still call him that out of respect.'

'But I don't even know him. How can I just start calling him "Uncle"?'

'You can't call him "Berris", like you and him are big alike. I want you to call him "Uncle" for now.' She laughed. 'You never know, if things work out maybe one day you'll call him "Dad".' Then came the killer. 'Jinx, Berris is having some problems where he lives. I told him he could stay here, with us, for a while, till he sorts something out.'

I'd been starving when I came in, famished enough to eat the whole dutchpot of curry on my own. But I'd been playing with my food as she spoke and somehow, even though I'd hardly eaten anything, my appetite was getting less and less the more she spoke.

'What, live here?' I asked.

'Yes.'

'Where? In the spare room?'

'He can sleep in my room,' she said with yet another laugh. 'In my bed. With me.'

I put my cutlery down as she rose from her side of the table and walked over to me. She bent down and cuddled me, then kissed me on the head. She was playing me, and I knew it. This was the kind of thing I normally did to her when I wanted money or clothes or for her to grant me a favour of some kind. What kids were supposed to do to parents, not the other way round.

'Don't worry, it's only for a while. You won't even know he's here. Okay?'

I was very unhappy about it. Very unhappy indeed. But what could I say? And it wasn't really like she was asking me because she had already told him he could stay. It was a done deal.

'Okay.'

She smiled at me and kissed me on the forehead again, smoothed my brows and flicked something from my hair.

'Good girl. Now eat up.'

There are many different types of rain, and England is famous for all of them. There are showers that start with a light drizzle, then build up to a steady pour. Then there's rain that begins drip drip, gets heavy, then stops then starts and stops and starts again. Then there's sudden rain that falls quickly when it's sunny, like its only ambition is to make a rainbow and once it's done that, it stops. If I had to describe Berris as rain, he was none of those, and the words 'You won't even know he's here' turned out to be the understatement of the year.

He moved in within days of my mother telling me and it was like he'd taken over completely, starting with the bathroom. There he spread his man-wares, things alien to our house till then: razors, shaving cream, Pearlwhite toothpaste,

Stud, Bay Rum, Brylcream and masses of bottles of after-shave too numerous to count. And he left bits of his jewellery everywhere. There were pieces around the sink, on the edge of the bath, on the cistern at the back of the toilet, the win-dowsill; Krugerrands and sovereigns on fat rings and heavy belchers, and his collection included some of the chunkiest chaparritas I'd ever seen in my life.

He had a toothbrush that was only a fraction smaller than the toilet brush, as though he needed an industrial cleaner or something to get rid of the gunk growing inside his whop-ping male gob. Even worse was the toilet seat that either had drips of his wee all over it that you had to wipe off before you could sit down, or was left up, in which case you had to try not to touch the wee on it when you were putting it back down so you could sit.

In the shower he had more lotions and potions than me and my mother put together: bottles of shower gel, Brut and All Spice, and an 'intimate wash' for his willy alone which was too gross to even think about. There were scrapers for the heels of his dry feet, tweezers for plucking the Yeti hairs from his nostrils, and a huge scratchy strap type of thing that was apparently the only thing in the universe that cleaned his back properly.

And clothes? There were masses of them. He was the living boutique. I swear he owned about twenty coats in every colour you could dream of and it seemed like every single one had a hat or cap to match it. And shoes? He must have had fifty pairs: leather shoes, suede shoes, patent shoes, lizards, snake skin, crocodile skin, *ostrich* skin for crying out loud, all of which I was forbidden to touch, and cleaning them seemed to be his number-one hobby.

The first thing my mother bought after he moved in was a huge wardrobe just for his stuff, but it wasn't enough. They spilled over into the wardrobe in the spare room and, over time, spread till they covered the bed completely. In fact, after a while it was like the spare room had become his personal walk-in wardrobe. Had we had a guest, there wasn't a space inside that room they could've sat never mind slept.

But the changes were much vaster than him and his clothes. They included the things I was used to and virtually everything I'd come to take for granted in my home. For example, before he came, my mother cooked what *we* liked, and that was chicken. Chicken and rice and peas, chicken curry, roast chicken, chicken soup, fried chicken. After he came, she was cooking for him: hard food instead of rice, boiling oxtail and butterbeans for hours on end, fried fish, fish soup, cow-foot and evil bubbling mannish water.

And suddenly, but kind of casually, like it had been happening my whole life, my mum began to serve up puddings after dinner. I was accustomed to puddings after lunch at school, but puddings *at home*? Before he came it would have been like chucking money down the drain. But suddenly, every meal had a pudding to follow it; apple pie and custard, rhubarb crumble, trifle, butterscotch-flavoured Angel Delight, treacle sponge pudding and home-made rum-and-raisin ice cream with cinnamon finely grated over the top.

Unused to a big meal followed by a hefty pudding, half the time I couldn't eat it. But Berris, he ate like it was his last supper every time; wolfed down those puddings like he had never tasted anything finer. Probably he hadn't. I wouldn't think many people had.

But the worst thing, the thing that got me most, was the evenings. Before Berris moved in, me and my mum would often stay up late watching TV: *Soap*, *Dallas* and *Dynasty*, *The Love Boat* and *Fantasy Island*. We were addicted to our weekly ration of other people's lives and dramas and even if one of us fell asleep, the other person made sure they stayed awake so they could fill in what had been missed. But after Berris came, the three of us would settle down in the living room, and all would be fine for about an hour or so. Then Berris would get up and say he was going to bed. About twenty minutes later, my mother would yawn loudly, as if suddenly overcome by fatigue. She would stretch and get up and say something about how tired she felt and go off to bed too. One time Berris actually went to bed at seven-thirty and she was just so exhausted she just couldn't keep her eyes open any longer come eight!

Everything changed when he came. *Everything*. I couldn't sleep in my mother's bed any more, because he was in there every night. Suddenly, I wasn't allowed to 'just bust' into her room, I had to knock first, and not just knock, I had to wait till it was convenient for them to *invite* me in. In my own home.

Every day I waited to hear that he'd sorted his situation out and would be moving on. I even checked his stuff for signs he'd started to pack, but there was nothing. It felt like it was *his* house and *I* was the visitor.

Berris wasn't a gradual drip drop of rain, an off-and-on downpour. It was like on a sunny summer's day there had been a sudden thunderclap, followed by a lightning flash and monsoon rain that poured without break, heavy, depressing, persistent, with no end in sight.

About six weeks after he'd moved in with us, one night after he'd gone to bed, when she yawned and stretched and stood up, that night, I'd had enough.

'How much longer is it gonna take him to find somewhere to live?' I asked. He was always 'him'. I would not call him 'Uncle' and I could not call him 'Berris' and I preferred to die rather than call him 'Daddy', so I called him nothing. She seemed surprised, as though living with him was just The Bomb for everyone.

'Why?' she asked. 'What's wrong with him being here? We've got the space. He's no problem...'

'No problem for you!' I shouted. 'I don't actually want to spend all my time in bed.'

I heard the crack of a slap before I realized she'd struck me, and I was stunned. There was a delay of a few seconds before I felt the sting across my cheek, and in that moment I could tell from her face, her surprise was equal to mine. She had never slapped me before. Never. And to do it over that man! I was more upset about that than the pain. I began to cry.

'I hate him. I don't want him here. This is Daddy's house, not his.'

An even more amazing thing happened then. I knew she'd surprised herself with the slap, so I was expecting her to comfort me, to turn back into the person I knew. Instead it was the opposite, she went further, becoming a stranger before my very eyes. Maybe she'd been changing for weeks and this was the first time I'd noticed, but I realized then. Suddenly I saw a strength in her I hadn't known existed. She pulled herself up to her full height, and looked at me steadily, coldly. The movement of her mouth when she spoke was exaggerated, like she was determined that even if I couldn't hear the words I would be able to lip-read them.

'This is *my* house,' she said. 'I say who comes and goes, and when. Berris lives here now. I hope I never have to have this conversation with you again.'

5

'S'funny thing to watch a person die. When you mum died, was out of the blue and there was things I shoulda said but I never, things I wished I'da told her but I didn't, and I have to say for years afterwards, man, that troubled me.

'I kept on saying if only I had the time back, and the knowledge I have now, I woulda done this for certain, I woulda said that for sure, woulda come clean for true and if I hadda done, maybe I coulda been happy. But Mavis taught me different. You don't just need the right time, have to be that in you mind, *you* in the right place too. And that's where you start in on the problem.

'When Mavis was ill, when we knew for sure she was gonna die, when I watched her getting smaller by the day no matter what I cooked and fed her, that was the time to talk, to clear my mind of the worries I'd had the whole of my marriage, put them straight once and for all, but I couldn't. It was the right place, but it felt like the wrong time. Hardly slept at all them last three months, tossing and turning like a fishing boat on top a rough sea, wondering what the best way was to put it; the best way to ask you dying wife, after you marry thirty-three years, if her thirty-two-year-old son was truly mine, just how to phrase it so's it wouldn't upset her.

'Upset her so much during her lifetime, did so many wicked things no other woman apart from Mavis woulda tolerate, yet she did. Knowing she was dying, I had no right to say a thing to add to the pile of all she already forgived me for, not a shred of right, not a ounce or drop. I wanted to ask more than anything. I *needed* to know. But I just couldn't do it. Couldn't bring myself to hurt her a single time more. In the end I swore to myself I would let it lie, leave all alone. I promised myself them words would never pass my lips. I would only do, I said, what needed to be done and say what she needed to hear me say and that was that.

'But that question ate at my belly same way the tumour ate at hers. Never give me no rest, man. We talked some talk. Most of it about back home. Talked about them twenty-odd years we growed up there. Talked about everything under the sun, even down to lipstick.' Lemon laughed, looking relaxed for a moment, swept along on the stream of his memories.

I lay there, watching him as he spoke without a glance in my direction, staring out into space. He could have been talking to me or to the room or to God. At some point, he picked up the tail end of what he had been saying and carried on as if there hadn't been a pause at all.

'When we was young men, boys really, when I first met Mavis, her lips was red. They had a flower back home, don't recall the name of it, but kinda like hibiscus. Folks used to call them "yellow flower". The girls used to take time to open them, peel back the petals careful like, one by one, fretting and watching in case was a bee inside. You ever see a black bee? I'm not talking about no bumblebee. Them black bees don't bumble, they fly like dragonflies, fast you see. And I tell you, them would soon as look at you as sting you. They was always round the yellow flowers, so the women had to be careful for true.

'Inside the petals was what we used to call "the male part", covered in a thick red powder. You rub you finger over the power then you rub it over you lips and that was lipstick. That was what all the girls wore then. That was the lipstick Mavis did have on the first time I clap eyes on her: yellow-flower red. When I try to remember her then, seems all I can see is her mouth and her teeth, pretty man, well pretty. She talked about yellow flowers, and school and the licks we used to get, and going to river, and mangoes. Man we eat some mangoes growing up. Eat mango till we have to go lie down. This is the kind of talk Mavis talk, recalling every tiny detail, while I feed her ice chips and press the flannel with little cool water on top her head, and all the while inside, that question was gnawing and gnawing away: *Tell me, Mavis, did some-one else kiss those yellow-flower red lips before me? Did you pass off another man's child all these years? Is John truly my son?'*

He lit another cigarette and inhaled deeply, settling back on the settee beside me. I was getting used to his way of just stopping in the middle of the tale as if he were finished.

I resisted as long as I could, then, 'So?' I said. 'Did you? Ask?'

He shook his head. 'Couldn't. Wanted to so bad, but I couldn't do it. Them last weeks, she hardly spoke at all. Just *thank you*. And *I love you*. Then, two days before she died, she said it. Two words. Opened her eyes – was the only part I could still say for sure was her, the eyes, the only part the cancer couldn't manage and left behind. Seemed like she was calling me, and I put my ear to her lips and she said, "He's yours." That's all. *He's yours*. Didn't need to say who she meant 'cos we both knew. I never said a word to her but still she heard me, heard me asking. With her dying breath, she told me what I wanted to hear but was never man enough to voice...'

'Oh my God,' I said. Maybe the alcohol had made me hypersensitive, because this had to be the saddest tale I had ever heard.

'I couldn't even speak, was so choked. Just cried. And held her hand while she close her eyes and slept again.'

My head was woozy. I was listening to him, listening to the inflection in his tone, and though I wasn't sure my judgement was sound, it seemed he was not yet finished. He had wanted to know the truth, after thirty-three years no less, and she had told him. So why didn't it sound like the story was drawing to a close? Why did it not sound like the end?

'But?' I asked.

'The thing is this: I know Mavis love me. Can't say why but she did. Have to accept that, 'cos she never give me reason to doubt it. Was times when I rave all night Saturday, pass the day in other women's yard and come home late Sunday night after I know she gone a bed. And my dinner was always there, dished and cover up on the side waiting; no questions, no blame, not a word. She k*new* me. Like a mother know her child. And no matter what blame was mine, she still go out of her way to make things all right for me, to please me. That was the problem.'

'I don't get you,' I said.

'I know Mavis woulda never said anything to me to upset me because she never did. Never. So even though she said it, I know she coulda say so *not* because it was true, but because she know it's what I needed to hear, and she give me with her dying breath what she give me with her living life, a plaster, a kiss to make things better and stop me bawling. In hospital, them call it a plessi-bow...'

I shook my head. 'I don't want to hear any more...'

'I knew Mavis would give me that lie 'cos she knew I needed it.'

'Why couldn't you just believe her?'

'And I took it. And wept. The last time she open her eyes, I gave her back a lie from the depths of my heart, I searched and found it and gave it back. The last words to ever pass from my mouth to her ears, the killer lie to beat all lies, one last big one to grease her passage to Calvary. She open her eyes and saw me where I sat 'side the bed waiting with her. I pick up her hand, looked her straight in the face, give her one last kiss and I said, "I believe you".'

He looked at me. He wanted something from me. Wanted it bad. But I was too overcome by sadness to work out what it was.

'Was I wrong?' he asked.

'I can't judge you,' I answered. 'It's not my call.'

'You know what you think though, don't you?'

'What I think doesn't matter.'

He wouldn't let it go. 'It matters to me.'

I was surprised to find I felt so strongly about this woman, his wife, a total stranger. Whether he believed her or not was his business. Yet even though I knew that, I was angry with him. That he had taken Berris's word over hers. That he had allowed Berris to ruin his marriage and offered no resistance whatsoever.

'You should have believed her.'

Instantly, his eyes were filled with tears and he sniffed, looked away from me and sniffed again. A speck of blood appeared on the floor at his feet, then another. He cupped his hands below his nose as the blood began to pour.

'I need a tissue,' he said, and I jumped up and ran.

He was a difficult patient. He refused to lie down in bed and insisted he would clean up the settee and the floor himself as soon as the bleeding stopped. I helped him up the stairs to the bathroom, and when we got there he closed the door and locked me out. I cleaned up anyway, and when he came back down, holding a wad of toilet paper beneath his nose, and realized, he kissed his teeth.

I had to virtually force him to sit down on the settee (again he refused to lie) and to lean his head back to slow the flow. He seemed unsurprised; clearly this was not the first nose-bleed he had ever had, and he was adept at dealing with it, in an obstinate kind of resentful way. He refused tea and coffee and paracetamol, insisting the only thing he needed was another drink.

I made it for him, fretting, convinced that more hard liquor, which he appeared to have been drinking non-stop since his arrival, was probably the last thing he needed. And when he took a mouthful, with his customary wince as it went down, I wondered whether he had some kind of alcohol-related illness or whether he was drinking more because he had some other medical problem and was of the opinion it no longer mattered what he did. Had he come to see me because he was putting his house in order while he still had time? As I had learned, the fact a person was too young to die did not buy them any more time. Was he dying?

I sat away from him, in the wicker chair opposite, watching, gauging that the bleeding had almost stopped, thinking his skin colour looked less natural, more like the pallor I was accustomed to working with, stupefied by the realization that the thought of Lemon dying hurt, genuinely hurt; that there was a chink in the armour of indifference that I'd been enveloped in for years.

I felt it.

But I was no closer to telling him anything. He had told me heaps. More than I had asked for. Much more. Yet, so far, I had shared nothing. He was right, you couldn't just pick up a piece out of a story and present it on its own. Alone, it was worthless. But I had not spoken to anyone ever about that night, had never trusted anyone enough to tell them the truth about what happened with my mother. I hadn't wanted to.

And now that I did want to, it seemed an impossible task. He didn't need to know about Sam and her family and the garages and Donovan. I wasn't his kind of storyteller, taking everything back to the dawn of time, slowly building up to the point chapter by chapter. This man was indecent. The choices he had made were beyond understanding, but the heinousness of them, the shamelessness, his disgraceful honesty, made him the one. It was either him or it would forever be no one. It *had* to be him. Maybe the beginning was wherever I chose it to be. It did not have to be Sam's spots, or meeting Berris. Maybe it had nothing to do with feet and where toes were pointing.

'I'm an embalmer,' I said.

'What's that?'

'I prepare the dead, so their families can see them. I work on people who have died, black people mostly, as a freelancer. Most of the funeral parlours round here use me. Probably because of the hair. They never know how to manage our hair. So they get me in and I do it, fix their hair and repair their faces, make them look comfortable, give their families back some peace. That's what I do for a living.'

'What kinda job is that?'

'I enjoy it,' I answered. I could not explain that it was the only thing I truly enjoyed, that among the dead was the only time I felt happy, that I was able to feel while I did my work: pride, vanity, grief, sadness, loss, *something*. That while I worked on those cold bodies, sometimes I found myself humming.

'Can't you get a job in some kinda beauty parlour instead?' he asked, and I laughed aloud.

'I could, but I don't want to.'

'Seems a strange way to make a living.'

'Someone has to do it. Someone did it for Mavis. Bet you appreciated it then.'

'It's no kinda life.'

'It's the only life I have.'

'It ain't...normal.'

'It suits me.'

I wanted him to link my work to *her*. It was an obvious link, but I needed him to make the connection himself. Then I could explain it was some kind of atonement and tell him why. I waited.

'You better not be planning to get them hands on me,' he said.

Despite my disappointment, I laughed again. 'I can wait.'

'Good,' he said, but he shook his head slowly for a long time afterwards and I knew he was disappointed too. He wanted more for me and I knew it would have been impossible to make him understand that for most of my adult life there had been nothing more that I wanted, nothing more that I needed, nothing more.

I put the TV on, sat back down beside him, and watched it in silence. Or at least I acted like I was watching it, face fixed resolutely in the direction of the screen. It felt strange, the close proximity, the sharing of the sofa, the evening. It reminded me of the years I'd spent watching TV in this same spot on another settee, with my mother, just us two; easy years, carefree times. I found myself more relaxed than I could remember being in a long time. And when he casually slipped his arm around me, over my shoulders, and pulled me closer so I was leaning into his warmth, I didn't resist or pull away. I snuggled up against him as my son had done, and felt just like a child.

In silence he held me, gently rubbing the top of my arm with his warm palm and I felt safe. For the first time since she had gone.

I felt it.

Though I was no closer to telling him the terrible truth, I felt okay and I was grateful. I knew it was merely a lull, the calm before the storm, yet his being there with me made me feel like maybe, somehow, there was a chance, the smallest suggestion of a hope, that things might turn out okay.

She made saltfish and Johnnycakes for breakfast. We'd never had it for breakfast on a weekday before, because the saltfish needed to be soaked overnight and boiled two or three times before it was ready to be used. And her Johnnycakes were a slow job, requiring sifting and kneading and frying on a low flame, to ensure that the outside didn't cook while the middle was still doughy, and by the time the middle cooked, the outside wasn't burned. It was a Special Treat, one we'd normally have for breakfast on Christmas Day or at Easter, and always on my birthday because, as we both knew, saltfish and Johnnycakes was my favourite breakfast.

We both also knew she'd cooked it because of the slap.

She must have gotten up at the crack of dawn to have it ready before I left for school, and I was glad – glad she'd recognized that what she'd done was weird and wrong, and even more glad that it had kept her awake, gnawed away, forced her out of the warm bed she now shared with Berris and into the kitchen at a time of day when those with clear consciences were still hard and fast asleep.

I ate without speaking, swallowing bulky mouthfuls slowly, pretending not to watch as she packed up Berris's precious portions into a couple of Tupperware containers for his lunch.

She kept up a perpetual flow of conversation, about the quality of saltfish on sale down Ridley Road Market, how it was best to buy a whole fillet rather than the pieces cut to fit the small packets they were usually sold in, because after you boiled what saltfish was inside them, then skinned and boned it, there was often hardly any actual fish left and by the time you finished cooking, there was nothing in the pot but onions.

She was wearing a dressing gown, slinky satin, in a dark gold colour, one I hadn't seen before. Underneath, she wore a matching nightie that was so short, when she moved and the gown opened over her legs, it looked as though she was completely naked till you caught a glimpse of the hemline, high up, more like a piece of underwear than something to keep you warm at night. I wondered where it had come from. Had *she* bought it or had *he*? What had she done with all her old nighties and pyjamas? When you started living with a man, did you need a whole new wardrobe of bedwear?

When Berris came in to collect his packed lunch, he was dressed casually in jeans and a black polo neck, hurrying because some other guy who worked with him at the Lesney factory gave him a lift in the mornings and he couldn't make him late. He still found time though, when she kissed him

goodbye, to put his hand on her bum, run it over the irresistible silky smoothness and give it a squeeze that made her
jump and then style it out like no one knew she'd swallowed
a shriek. She laughed and wriggled away from him, glancing
over at me where I sat staring at my plate like it was the telly.
A moment later he was gone and I felt my confusion beginning to clear. She owned this house and he owned her. The
only thing I needed to get my head around was where exactly
I fitted in.

'I thought maybe we could go out later,' she said. 'After
school. I'll come by and meet you and we can go down
Kingsland Road, do a bit of shopping. Would you like that?'

She knew me and she knew I would like that very much.
To me it was kind of like I knew she was sorry for slapping
me and that she was doing her best to make up for it, but
while I knew that and felt sorry for her, I just couldn't bring
myself to act like it hadn't happened or I'd forgotten or things
were cool, so I shrugged as if it was no big deal.

When she tried to put her arm around my shoulders I stood
up quickly, lifting my plate and stepping away from the table.
I turned my head to the side when she went to kiss me so that
she almost kissed the air beside my cheek.

'See you later,' I said, without looking at her.

Walking up the road to meet Sam, I wondered why it was
that *I* was the one who'd been left feeling bad.

'Only reason it even seems like anything big is 'cos you don't
get regular beats,' Sam said. We were in the toilets at first
break, in front of the mirror. She had both her mouth and

her right eye opened into an O and, when she talked, it was without moving her lips. She held a tube of mascara in one hand and was using the other to apply the make-up to her lashes. 'If you lived in my yard, you'd know something about beats.'

'Yeah, but ain't it worse if you never get hit, to then get slapped for no reason?' I asked. Sometimes she was so annoying. It was like whatever was going on with you was always small fry. She'd already experienced it on a much bigger scale and your titchy problem was nothing compared to what she'd been through.

'Yeah, but what did you think she would say when you started going on about sex?'

'I never said nothing about sex!'

'Oh? Like they're really going bed that early 'cos they're just so tired. *Every* night. I've told you, black people are more sexed than white people. What did you think they were doing?'

Suddenly, it was clear to me that she was right. No wonder she sometimes talked to me like I was some kind of idiot. Had my mum thought when I'd said 'bed' that I was talking about sex too?

'Sam, just forget it,' I said.

She was blinking fast in front of the mirror now.

'They're at it big time, boy, night after night, like rabbits...'

'Puh-lease!'

'I know for a fact your mum ain't wearing no costume at night.'

'Why would she be doing that?'

'S'what you have to do if you don't want more kids. Especially if you're with a black guy. My mum's got three.'

'Your mum's got *three* swimming costumes?'

'Yep. She always wears them. Under her nightie. Every night. You telling me your mum ain't got none?'

I sifted through her wardrobe of nightwear old and new in my head, and shook it.

'Then don't be surprised if any day now you hear the patter of little feet.'

I didn't want to talk to Sam about my mum having sex. I didn't even want to think about it.

'Sam, I beg you, shut up right now or I'll kill you!' I snatched the tube of mascara out of her hand, whipped out the brush and brandished it at her, slipping my feet into a fencing position, like d'Artagnan from *The Three Musketeers*. 'With this!'

She looked at the brush, looked at me, and raised her eyebrows.

'Jay, you're really scaring me, man.'

She snatched it out of my hand as the bell went. We began to make our way back to class.

'I got asked out again last night,' she said casually, like she'd only just remembered. She'd gone to the garages after school yesterday on her own again. For years everything we'd done we'd done together. Every interest we had was shared. We'd talked about boys, but they were outside of us and the things we did. But recently, something had changed in her, like us being together wasn't enough any more, playing with our hair, running jokes, passing notes, swapping

Mills & Boons, all those things we'd done a thousand times, that I wanted to do a thousand more, she now called 'dry'. She wanted excitement, the unknown, more. Increasingly, it felt like she had a double life, the one she shared with me, and another separate world over the garages. At first she used to tell me everything that went on there. Now she specially selected bits to tell me and I found myself endlessly trying to work out how much of what she'd told me was true and what had been left out. For some reason it all felt kind of seedy to me. According to Sam, that was because I was too stuck-up, or to use her word, *stush*.

'Who by?'

'Donovan, innit.'

'And?'

'Blatantly it ain't happening.'

'Why are you so wicked to him?'

'I ain't ready for no big-time relationship. I'm young, man. I've got my whole life ahead of me and I wanna have some fun. I ain't tying myself down. I'm gonna be a air hostess or a actress and I don't want no big ole black ole weight holding me back, bawling every time I'm getting on a plane, breeding me down.'

'Did you tell him that?'

'I said I'd think about it. He's gonna be over the garages later. You have to help me decide how I'm gonna blow him out. You *are* coming, aren't you?'

'I can't,' I said. 'My mum's meeting me from school.'

'Jay, you know what? If you let them, parents will fuck up your life for good,' she said.

*

Of course, there was no sign of that opinion when we walked out of the school gates to find my mum leaned up against the barrier waiting for me. She looked good, slim and attractive and well dressed, young in comparison with the parents of the other kids. Even so I felt kind of sheepish, but Sam was straight in there with *Hello, Mrs Jackson. I'm very well, thank you. Yes they're all fine. I'd love to come with you, but I've got my own chores waiting for me.* Then with a quick wink at me and a pat of her hair, she was on her way.

My mum and I went shopping down Ridley. She bought me two pairs of leg warmers and a wicked pair of Levis. Then we went to a café near the bottom of the market and ordered dinner, just us two, like in the old days, before Him.

Normally, it would've been a real treat being there, but I felt awkward sitting opposite her. It had been easier not speaking while we were moving and the market was bustling around us, but now it was just us and the silence that came from my end and drowned out her attempts to make up.

Then out of the blue she just said it.

'I shouldn't have slapped you. It was wrong and I'm sorry. I was angry, but that doesn't make it okay. I won't do it again.'

For some weird reason my eyes filled with tears.

'Jinxy, I know this is hard for you. I know that. You've had me to yourself nearly your whole life, and now you have to share. I understand that. But you have to try and understand as well. One day, you're gonna leave…'

'No I won't.'

She smiled. 'You will. You'll grow up and fall in love with someone wonderful and you'll want to be with them and you'll go. Would you have me sitting on my own in that big old house, lonely and crying? No one to talk to, no one to laugh with, no one to hold me?'

I did understand, although the 'hold me' bit was embarrassing. I knew what she meant and I knew she wasn't being unreasonable, but I still said, 'It's not fair.'

'Talk to me,' she said. 'Tell me what I can do that would make things okay for you.'

What came to my mind was: *Chuck him out! Tip his stuff into the street! Let him go be tired in some other woman's house! Make everything as it was before!* I shrugged my shoulders and she sighed.

'I love him,' she said, when I had most wanted her to say she loved me. 'I love him and he is a part of my life now...part of *our* lives. But it doesn't change anything between us, me and you. I will always be here for you. Do you believe me?'

My throat was so choked I thought my voice would break. 'Yes.'

She reached over the table and held my hand, squeezing it firmly enough to make me look at her, but not enough to hurt. 'That is my promise to you for all time. I will always be here for you.'

'I believe you,' I said. She let go of my hand as our plates arrived. I wiped my eyes as though I was just flicking off a speck that had randomly landed on my lashes. 'This looks good,' I said and smiled at her. She returned the smile and we ate.

*

It was after seven by the time we returned back home. I was happy we'd gone out together, that we'd managed to sort things out. I was determined to try harder to be understanding of Berris even though I didn't want him there, because she *did* want him there and she was my mum and he made her happy, and somehow I had to find a way to make the best of it.

But he was vexed.

He hardly looked at her when we came in. He was in the living room, just sitting on the settee, not playing music or watching TV. I wondered if he'd been standing at the window watching out for us coming down the street. He acted like we'd done something wrong, but I didn't know what that was. My mother didn't know either, I could tell. She made light of it, pretending she hadn't noticed his mood, kissing his cheek and making jokes like he was happy and joking back with her. When he looked at me, I saw something in his eyes that I understood, and it surprised me. It had been the first time since he'd moved in that she'd spent any time with me on my own, two or three hours on one occasion in nearly two months, that was all.

And he was jealous.

To me he was acting like a child who was angry with his friend for liking someone else as well. His lips were pursed, he wouldn't meet her eyes or speak. He met mine though, and the message in them was clear: he was upset and it was my fault. I couldn't do the chirpy acting my mum was styling out like she was aiming for an Oscar, and in the end, after all the complaining I'd done about the two of them going to bed early, I ended up leaving them in the living room, for the first time the first to go to bed. I said that I was tired and went upstairs to my room.

I lay in bed, on my back, a Mills & Boon propped open against my knees, and I would have been reading it if it had been possible to concentrate. But I couldn't. I could hear them. Arguing. I couldn't hear the details, but I could hear the pitch of their voices. His was angry. Accusing. Hers was placatory. Pleading. At some point I was sure she was crying.

I got off the bed and went over to the door, opening it slightly, still standing inside my room, able to hear a bit better, alarmed but unable to decide if I should go downstairs or stay in my room and carry on pretending I couldn't hear a thing. Suddenly I heard my mum cry out, loudly, as if she'd been hurt. It went quiet then for what felt like a very long time and my indecision felt like a pressure building up inside me. I heard someone come up the stairs and go into the bathroom and close the door. The footsteps were hasty and clumsy.

Berris.

I waited a few minutes longer, scared he would come straight back out and catch me, but he didn't. Finally, I forced myself to move my feet and they carried me down the stairs.

I walked into the kitchen and, to my surprise, he was sitting there, at the table on his own, eating leftover Johnnycakes and saltfish; waxing it off.

He looked up at me in that strange way I was still getting used to, not actually meeting my eyes, just kind of focusing on me in bits; firstly my hair and then my breasts, then nodded in the direction of my feet before his eyes went back to his plate. I didn't know whether he'd been greeting me, or if I'd just been dismissed.

There was something about him at that particular moment which disturbed me, but it was hard to put my finger on it exactly. It was as if he had a glow around him, not the visible one around the kids in the Ready Brek advert, more of an aura I couldn't see but felt instead, something physical and static and scary. I didn't like him, I knew that. But it wasn't just dislike I felt, it was fear, the kind of fear you experienced passing a digi group of bullies when you were on your own. His eyes had that same look about them that I'd seen in the eyes of bullies, not just threatening, but smug too, like he knew something that gave him power over anyone who was weaker. It made me feel afraid.

'Where's Mum?' I asked, looking around the kitchen, though it was obvious she wasn't there.

'Upstairs in her room,' he said and he flicked his head towards the ceiling, like he was saying *Up there* and at the same time telling me he couldn't care less. I waited for a second, but he didn't look back up.

'Thanks,' I said, relieved to be leaving the room and more worried than I had been before I had entered.

She was still inside the bathroom and though the door was closed it was unlocked, so I tapped first and when she didn't answer, opened it and saw her, bent over the sink with the cold tap running. She was splashing water on to her face.

'Mum?'

She turned her head to look at me.

'Oh my God,' I said and she turned away quickly and started squeezing out the flannel in the sink, carefully folding it and gently dabbing at her face. I took a step closer, watching her movements through the mirror above the bowl. The left side of her face was bruised, from the eye – puffed up so bad it could hardly open – to the cheekbone. Against her pale skin, the bruising was a riot of colours, a deep maroon giving way to dark red giving way to crimson round the edges. And in the centre, a gash about an inch long bled.

'It's all right,' she said in a chatty kind of tone, talking well fast, 'it looks worse than it feels. Don't start fretting, Jinx. I'm really fine.'

Downstairs the front door slammed. I assumed it was Berris, leaving. As if that was her cue, she sagged to her knees, covered her face with her hands and I stood dumbstruck beside my mother as she started to cry.

He'd done it. I knew in my stomach it was him, but when I tried to ask her about it she fobbed me off, and when I pushed it she started getting angry, so I ended up backing off and though it was the most traumatic thing that had ever happened in our house, we didn't discuss it.

But even though I wasn't putting my thoughts into words, I couldn't get the questions out of my head. Like, what could make a big man like Berris punch my mother in the face? How could he have looked at my beautiful mum and done that, then calmly sat downstairs and eaten? From what I saw, she did everything he wanted, tried her hardest to be perfect for him. I could think of nothing she could've done or said that made sense of how he'd manhandled her.

Maybe she was right when she said I was too young to understand. Maybe that was true. But the way she cried, the level of her upset, I was sure she was no clearer on the answers to those questions than I was.

We stayed up together till late that night, like old times, me sat beside her on the settee watching TV, her arms around my shoulders, kissing my head from time to time, silently wiping away the tears that just refused to stop coming, while I acted like I never saw them. She wasn't watching the telly really and neither was I. We each pretended for the other's sake that everything was perfectly normal, ho hum, when it was clear the whole world had violently tipped and life as we knew it was upside down; each of us pretending neither had our ears cocked for the sound of his return, that neither of us was dreading it.

It was after twelve when we finally went to bed, yet late as it was I couldn't go to sleep. I felt too confused, as if I'd been battered myself. Confused by all the feelings inside me that had nowhere to go, but still boiled and bubbled furiously like mutton inside a pressure cooker.

I wanted to kill him. I'd been angry before in the past, but nothing on this scale ever. I wanted him dead. My heart bled for her, but for him I prayed for a double-decker bus to mow him down that very same night, to splatter his carcass across the high street in a dead, flat mass. I hated him.

Yet beneath that, to my shame, and I would have rather died than admit it to anyone, beneath that, I was glad. It was clear to me he'd messed up big time. The single bright light that shone for me that night was that he'd gone too far. He'd hurt my mum in a way that was beyond understanding. What he had done, she'd never forgive. I'd wanted him out of our lives and, with his bad-tempered self, he'd handed it to me on a plate. After what he'd done, the relationship was over; I knew beyond any doubt that now and for all time she'd never take him back.

It would probably take a while for her to get over it, but once she did, things could return to normal and I would, as I'd wanted all along, have my mum back to myself. We would be happy, the two of us, the way we were before he came. And it was that comforting thought alone that made it possible for me to relax enough to finally get some sleep.

I brought her breakfast in bed. Tea and toast with scrambled eggs, arranged on a tray beside a love heart I'd cut out and coloured in myself to cheer her up. With him gone, I didn't have to knock. Still I entered her room on tiptoe, so as not to wake her. But on that score, I needn't have worried at all.

She was lying under the bedspread, on her side, eyes open, staring at nothing, and I wondered if she'd managed to get any sleep at all that night, because she looked wrecked.

She smiled and sat up, trying to act like everything was still cool, but it wasn't and I knew it. She was treating me like a baby, like I wasn't old enough for her to tell me stuff, so young and stupid in fact that if she pretended hard enough, I wouldn't be able to guess there was anything wrong at all. And it struck me as weird really, because not only did I feel older, but it felt as though everything was reversed and some-how I'd become the mum and she was now the child.

'Aren't you going to school?' she asked.

'It's just revision. It's okay. I won't miss anything.'

Normally there'd have been no way she would have let me skip school for no good reason. But I think she was too tired to make an issue of it. She must have known there was no way on earth I was going to go to school and just act like it was some regular, random day. How could I leave her alone in the state she was in?

She didn't eat much. In truth, I'd done a bit of a bodge-job. I'd been concentrating so hard on stirring the eggs that I forgot the toast under the grill and it had burned. By the time I scraped off the black bits it was cold and somehow, all the black bits managed to get into the butter, which didn't melt into the toast like it was supposed to, but just sat on top look-ing filthy. She was kind of humouring me with the few nibbles she had, but she didn't fancy it and I could hardly blame her. She drank most of the tea though, and smiled at me between sips, and picking up the heart, she looked at it, blinking fast, and touched my face and kissed me and said thanks.

Her eyes kept welling and spilling, despite the smiles. It felt like her heart was broken and the knowledge broke mine. I wanted her back to normal but I didn't know how to make that happen. I looked at the pathetic heart I had made. It had been childish of me to think a scrap of paper could change everything in a flash. How could it be possible for a tiny piece of paper to accomplish a massive thing like that? That day I learned a new kind of fear.

I ran her a bath and she lay in it for over an hour, hardly moving. I had to encourage her to get out and then all she wanted to do was just lie down and rest, like she hadn't already rested for most of the day. When I went to check on her at lunchtime to see if she wanted me to make her something else to eat she was fast asleep and, I had to admit it, I was relieved.

While she slept I cleaned up downstairs. I moved quickly, trying to keep ahead of the fear that dogged me. Not of Berris, but of her, how she was. It was like someone had shaken everything out of her, every ounce of hope, every decent memory, everything good she'd kept stored inside, and left in its place a sack, one that could still be shifted from place to place, propped up, made to lie flat, but no matter how hard I searched, was empty inside. It did my head in to see her like that, really did it in. What would happen if she stayed like that for good? Was it possible for someone to never recover from something like this? It was sick and it was selfish, but still I wondered, if she didn't recover, what would happen to me?

I took out some food and made dinner. I'd been watching my mother cook for years, marinating, seasoning, frying, boiling, stewing. In a baptism of fire, I went from scrambled eggs on toast to rice and peas and chicken. I discovered that what I had taken for granted, fine meals beautifully presented and tasting like heaven, was actually an art form my mother had perfected. It was tough, not just the chicken and the rice, but the whole process. Watching and doing were two different things. That was the second thing I learned that day.

I underestimated the time it took the red peas to cook and even though I'd boiled them for about an hour before I put the rice in, they were hard, rubbery edged with crunchy centres; and the rice was way overcooked, soggy as pudding. I turned the fire up under the pot to dry it out a bit and it burned at the bottom, leaving a distinctly smoky flavour, not yummy-smoked like sizzling bacon, more like the singe of overheated iron combs on hair.

But the chicken looked okay. I'd taken it out of the freezer and defrosted it under the running tap before seasoning it and putting it in the oven to roast. It looked a lot better than the gravy, which was pitch black from an overdose of gravy browning, and tasted well weird, more like a chemistry experiment gone wrong than anything I'd ever come across before on a dinner plate.

When it was ready, I carried her dinner up to her on a tray. I was relieved to see not only that she had gotten up but she was also dressed, sitting on the edge of her bed, painting her toenails. She broke into a smile when she saw the plate, which was good, though the laughter that followed was like the right sign in the wrong place. I went to get my own plate of food and we ate together in her room, something else we hadn't done in yonks.

I have to say the meal was despicable, and after the consolation I took from the chicken, which was the only thing on the plate that looked *nearly* okay, as soon as I cut into it, it began to bleed.

'Next time it will be better,' she said. 'Don't worry. When I was your age I didn't even know how to make a cup of tea.'

We took our plates back downstairs and emptied them and she helped me tidy up the mess I had made of the kitchen. She gave me some money and I left, headed for Kentucky's to buy us some finger-licking food it was actually possible to eat. She was up, she was moving, she was talking. I was so happy I wanted to fly. I bombed it all the way to Mare Street and then, so our food didn't get the chance to cool too much before we ate it, I bombed it back.

The round trip took about half an hour and I was out of breath as I opened the front door, calling out to her. She didn't answer. When I stepped inside the living room she was sitting on the settee looking down at her lap, demurely. Beside her sat a man I'd never seen before, tall and light-skinned, really good-looking for an old guy, and very smartly dressed. He smiled at me as I entered, real friendly like. It was so contagious that I smiled back automatically and the smile froze on my lips when I realized that Berris was in the room too, standing beside the window, his weight on one shoulder pressed hard against the wall, as if his legs alone were not strong enough to keep his body upright. His other hand was wiping away a stream of tears.

He looked at me. I think it was the first time he had ever looked me in the eyes for more than a few seconds, like he was so distraught he didn't care who saw him or what they thought, as if being that upset exempted him from pride and shame.

'This must be Jinx,' the other man said. 'I'm Berris' friend, Lemon.'

Looking at Berris, I experienced a feeling that I despised for years after. I'd never seen a grown man cry before. Never.

Up till then it was something I hadn't even known was possible. I must have read about forty Mills & Boon books all in all, and in not a single one had any man cried or even come close, whether they were sorry for what they'd done or not. And Berris looked like he had been crying non-stop for twenty-four hours straight. His eyes were red, the skin all around them puffed and swollen and blotchy. Even though his skin was dark, his nose was still blatant Rudolf.

I'd hated that man so bad for weeks, wanted nothing else in that time but that he pack up and get out of our home, yet he looked more wretched than any man, woman or child I'd ever seen in my life. Like he knew he'd done the worst thing a person could ever do and was truly, to the heart, sick and remorseful and sorry. He couldn't look at her and he couldn't stop himself from bawling like a baby. It was the most pathetic thing I'd ever seen.

In that moment, because I knew what he'd done, how he'd smashed in my mother's face in temper, because the memory of him polishing off his dinner and the look of pure satisfaction in his eyes was still fresh and vivid in my mind, my feelings shocked me. I looked at the man who had caused our family so much hurt, so much upset, and there was no denying it; I felt sorry for him.

I felt sorry for him.

6

It was the smell that woke me. Heaven scent. Both alien and familiar at the same time. First it permeated the air, then pervaded my nostrils, then made its way down to my gut where it took hold and wrenched hard, and I found myself simultaneously hungry and awake.

I lay where I had fallen asleep the night before, on the settee still. Lemon had put the blanket over me, wedged a pillow under my head, and I had slept like a babe. I didn't know where he had slept himself, but he was up now, in the kitchen, frying fish.

I could smell it.

Snappers maybe or red mullet. Traditional fare. The kind of fish my mother had fried, the kind of smell this house had not contained since that time. Maybe he intended to feed me to death, kill me with West Indian food, serve me every dish my mother had ever cooked and given me, bring back into this house everything that made me remember her and all those things I had foolishly thought I had been so successful in forgetting.

It smelled delicious.

I threw back the blanket and stood. It had been a long time since I'd had the pleasure of waking to a meal I hadn't prepared myself. I breathed in slowly, relishing the wonderful odour, realizing what I felt was more than mere hunger, it wasn't just a desire for something to pick at or nibble on: I was famished. Not only did I want to ingest the aroma, my mouth was salivating, my stomach contracting as though I hadn't eaten for weeks. The only time I could ever remember having that kind of physical response to food was when I had been pregnant with Ben, as though all sense of smell and taste had risen a plane, gone up a level, a hunger that was elevated to the realm of the supernatural. For a moment, my longing for the breakfast Lemon was cooking was so intense I actually felt afraid.

I folded up the blanket and took it upstairs with the pillow and had a shower. A fast one. And brushed my teeth and dressed and went back downstairs where I found him waiting for me, sitting on the second to bottom step. He stood up as I approached and nodded his good morning.

'I cooked breakfast,' he said.

'I know.'

'You ready for it now?'

'Yep.'

'Then come. We eat.'

I followed him.

I was right, it was red mullet, perfectly fried, crisp and salty on the outside, moist and steaming on the inside, served with a fiery salsa of onions, sweet and scotch bonnet peppers, tomatoes and garlic, and on the side of the plate, a small pile of cucumber, sliced wafer thin and smothered in lemon juice, pepper and salt.

'Is good?' he asked, watching me, his cutlery in his hands, his own plate as yet untouched.

My mouth was full so I nodded. I was eating slowly, exploring the tastes inside my mouth and the experience was as erotic as foreplay. I swallowed.

'Bloody good,' I said.

'You look like you could do with little meat on them bones.'

'Are you trying to fatten me up?'

'I'm just saying you don't need to be on no diet.'

'You're hardly Barry White yourself.'

'But I eat proper food.'

'*I* eat proper food.'

'Decent food.'

'Marinated overnight then cooked down for five hours?'

'With taste.'

'I have to admit, this is delicious, Lemon.'

'You look so much like her.'

'Don't spoil this for me,' I said.

He made sorrel. First sorting through the dried hibiscus flowers and discarding the bad ones, filling and refilling the kettle and pouring the boiled water into a mixing bowl that had been unused for almost a decade and a half. Then he tipped the flowers into the bowl, where they floated. He used a ladle to press them down into the water, where immediately they began to bleed.

I sat on the high stool and watched him.

The radio played soca in the background. Different parts of Lemon's body danced at different times; his bouncing shoulders, his nodding head, his tapping toes or winding waist or swivelling hips. At no time while he worked was he ever detached from the music. Even when he was grating fresh ginger into the mixture, he kept perfect time with the beat.

He threw in whole cinnamon sticks and a couple of cloves. With a knife he peeled the skin from a large orange in a single coiling strip and let it fall in. Then he halved and juiced a couple of lemons and added them as well. Last came the cane sugar and he poured in almost half the bag. The air was spicy and zesty, filled with the promise of tasty future treats.

'I can't remember when's the last time I had sorrel,' I said.

'I made this for Mavis once sometimes twice a week. Was one of her favourite drinks. And mine.'

He used a ladle to stir till the sugar was dissolved to his satisfaction. Finished, he turned the volume of the radio up and danced his way over to where I sat. He took my arm and tried to pull me to stand and dance but I resisted.

'I don't do calypso,' I said.

He continued dancing as if I had gotten up and was dancing with him, holding both my hands and moving them in time to the beat as he jumped and pranced and bounced his body against my legs and knees and thighs. It was impossible not to laugh, not to be swept upstream with him on the current of his exuberance, and as soon as I did he pulled me off the chair, and because it was pointless trying to resist any longer, I joined in. I couldn't remember the last time I had danced.

Afterwards, we put the telly on and he asked me to get the hair-grease and comb. He sat on the settee and I sat on the floor between his legs. Working in sections, he greased my scalp, then combed and plaited my hair in tiny perfect braids that were better than any I could have done myself. The last person to have done that was my mother. He was unhurried and so gentle. At one point I had to struggle to keep my eyes open it was that nice. And unexpected. I sipped sweet sorrel on a warm, full belly and found myself content.

'You did her hair as well, didn't you?' I asked, and he nodded. Then all was silent till he finished.

'You have any clippers?' he asked.

'Upstairs,' I yawned.

'Bring them down, and some cream.'

'What, *now*?'

'Unless you busy.'

I went upstairs to my bedroom, searched quickly, then brought them to him.

He clipped my fingernails, and filed them down. Then rubbed cream into my hands, slow and meticulous around the cuticles, so gently it was almost impossible to believe a man was doing it. Finished with my hands he did my feet. The nails first and then more filing. He took longer over creaming them, rubbing and squeezing and pressing and massaging them on their way into foot heaven. I sat on the settee looking down at him, watching as he worked, studying the careful precision of his fingers, marvelling that I had ever thought them clumsy, relaxing till it seemed I might slide off the settee into a shapeless, boneless heap of melted contentment at his feet. And still he rubbed.

With his fingers.

I was aroused.

He looked up at me and I wondered, did my breathing change? Had my temperature suddenly soared? I couldn't say precisely how, but I knew he knew exactly what I was feeling; he had always known, always. The words tumbled out of my mouth involuntarily.

'I love you.'

The movement of his hands slowed, almost to a stop.

'You don't know me.'

'I know enough.'

'You got no idea who I am, the things I've done.'

It wasn't what I wanted to hear. On the verge of tears I said, 'I don't care.'

He released my feet and stood. 'I shouldn'ta come.'

'Why won't anyone love me?' The tears began to fall and I hated them for coming now, for the indignity, but I had no more control over them than I had over the words queued up inside my throat. 'Not her! Not him! Not you! Not even my son! Why?'

'She did love you.'

'She didn't.'

'I know she did.'

'She loved him, only him. After he came there was nothing left for me. Nothing.'

'How can you think that?'

'I was there! I saw!'

'From what I seen, I know she loved you.'

'And you?'

'I don't have the right.'

'I give you the right.'

'You don't know enough to say that.'

I was shameless in my begging. *'Please!'*

'I'm sorry,' he said and reached his hands out as if he wanted to hold me, to embrace and comfort me. I chopped at his outstretched arms with one of my own as hard as I could, and with the other I wiped my face.

I said, 'In that case, keep your fucking hands to yourself!'

I felt like an idiot, a silly adolescent child. Like I was sixteen years old again. What was the point of time passing if nothing changed? I cleaned the bathroom. Wiped out the bath and the bowl and the shower. Then the mirror and every surface. And swept and mopped then dried the floor.

I was fuming. At myself. For wanting too much, for asking. For forgetting that I had loved him once before and had already been hurt. Furious that what I wanted to say was still bound tight inside me and I was blurting out the things that were better kept hidden. It was the food, and the drink, and the comfort, peeling back my armour to leave me naked. Instead of loving my son, I was loving this man who had already let me down, doing what my mother had done to me. I studied my face in the mirror seeking any sign that I had changed, or worse, seeking signs that I had changed into her.

He was in the kitchen when I went back downstairs, funnelling the last of the sorrel into empty bottles he must have retrieved from the recycling box outside. When he looked at me I wondered what he saw. *Who.* I wanted to say sorry, but unlike the declarations of love mobilized to burst their way free of my lips, the apology merely smouldered.

He smiled.

It was as simple as that.

He smiled and we were friends again.

'These will keep for weeks,' he said, indicating the bottles.

I nodded slowly as if that was an extremely useful thing to know.

'If you keep them in the fridge. They can prob'ly even freeze.'

'I'm sure I'll drink them before then.'

He looked away from me for a moment, to the side where his drink sat. He put his finger into the glass and swirled the ice around. He took the finger out and rubbed his hands together to rid them of the moisture.

'If you want me to, I'll go.'

'I don't want you to.'

'I don't know what I'm doing, why I bothered to come. I told myself it was for you, but that's not true. I never did nothing I didn't do for myself.'

'Join the club,' I said.

'I should be strong. What I have to tell you don't really make no difference after all this time. Only reason for telling you is that it might do some good for me.'

'Okay.'

'Thing is, I don't know where to start…'

'You've been talking for days. You've already started, haven't you?'

He smiled again. 'That's true. You right. Think I'm just stalling. I brought things to make Guinness Punch. You like it?'

'I do, but I'm running out of space in my fridge.'

'We'll drink it when I'm done.'

'Okay.'

He held his palms out towards me and said, 'I just need something to do with these hands.'

'Okay.'

'Only, I forgot the Nutrament. I'm gonna pop out and buy some. I won't be long.'

'Fine.'

I stood aside to let him pass, but he didn't move. My eyes met his and communication started.

'One last thing. You know you said nobody loves you?' he asked. Instantly my vision was blurred by tears and I nodded. 'Just think I prob'ly need to say that that's not true.'

7

The mirror I held in my hand was bigger than my head, yet it was too small to be able to see everything I wanted to see, to see all the things I needed to see in order to get my head around the things in my life that it was impossible to get my head around. Still, I looked.

Though it was a Thursday morning and I should have been leaving for school, my mum was pressing my hair. I could hear the iron comb sizzling, could smell the scorch as it passed through my nappy locks, magically transforming them into silken tresses that were straighter than when she'd started, closer to the coolie hair on her own head that she was able to take for granted.

The comb had to be blazing to do its job properly – not red hot, which would burn the hair off my head, but – in my view anyway – not much cooler. I sat on a chair beside the cooker, adjacent to the low flame of the front burner, watching her section and comb and press, holding the towel tight around my shoulders so my uniform wouldn't get messy, and each time the rising smoke cleared, I found myself examining her face.

If anything, that morning, the bruising looked worse. Overnight the redness had settled to black-greens and purpley-browns that glistened beneath the Vaseline she'd smoothed over it. I was trying to focus on watching what she was doing with my hair, tensed for the sear of the iron comb against my scalp, or worse – and more likely – the top tips of either ear, but my eyes and my thoughts were on *her*, trying my hardest to understand how it was possible for anyone to look so beat-up and yet so happy at the same time. And boy was she happy. She was so full of joy that day, she was glowing.

He was back.

It had been inevitable from the moment he dragged his sopping carcass into our living room. Even though I knew it was a waste of time, I had still harboured the faintest of hopes that he'd brought Lemon around to help him pack, but of course, he hadn't. Lemon had come to beg on Berris's behalf for my mother's forgiveness. His presence was needed to stop her phoning the police in a panic, thinking Berris had returned to the house to finish her off. He was there to act as a peacemaker, to keep the discussion calm, to hand Berris the occasional tissue, to keep me occupied so that the two of them could have privacy for their Big People Talk.

In the kitchen, Lemon asked for a cup of tea and I made it. He drank it while I slowly picked at the chicken and chips I'd such a short time ago been so excited about. I ate with indifference and Lemon talked all the while, real friendly like, friendlier than Berris had ever been, asking about school, my lessons, my teachers there. My answers were short, you could even say abrupt. I couldn't really concentrate enough on what he was saying to have a full-blown conversation. It's very hard to have a normal discussion with anyone when you have one ear cocked and your whole body braced to charge out of the room at the first sound of a scream.

I'd made my way through about half the box when my mother bounded into the kitchen.

Beaming.

When we'd left her, she'd been all eyes downcast, on the verge of tears herself, utterly miserable. When she came into the kitchen, neither of us needed to ask for a summary of how their talk had gone. She was happy and laughing, even as she winced from the pull of sore skin over bruising.

'We've sorted everything out,' she said, virtually singing the words, and I felt so many things that even if anyone had actually bothered to ask my opinion, I wouldn't have had a clue what to say.

I felt sorry for her because I'd seen first hand how much he'd hurt her, not just physically, but her spirit, her mind. I was glad for her that he was back in her life and abracadabra, she was happy again. And Berris? I hated him, hated what he'd done. At the same time I felt sorry for him, for the low level his wrongs had sucked him down to, and in a way relieved. His suffering over the last day had obviously been on par with hers. Maybe it really was true love. I felt relieved for him that things had been sorted out, that he could now fix himself up and carry himself with a little more pride.

Every time I thought of how he'd looked, how wet and snotty and pathetic, I squirmed inside.

But for myself, I was wretched. I wanted him here, I wanted him gone. I wanted her happy, I wanted her to myself. Round and round it all went inside my mind like a merry-go-round, till my head began to feel like it was me that had taken the pounding.

And afterwards, Lemon had left briefly, then come back again. He'd stayed late, the three of them laughing and drinking and eating and joking till after midnight. Must be as soon as the front door clicked closed behind his back, they were ready for bed. Then this morning she was up early, fixing Berris a hearty breakfast before he went to work, hugging me, fussing over my hair, pressing it on a Thursday morning before school, a process that took ages and was normally done on a Sunday night. She had a strange smell about her that I'd noticed before but couldn't identify, like the smell on her hands sometimes, hours after she'd been chopping onions. Not quite that smell, but like it. I felt again as I had yesterday, like I was the responsible adult and she was a kid who'd been naughty and was going to extra lengths to smooth things over.

'I don't want you to worry,' she said. 'All relationships have their ups and downs. And anyway, Berris never actually meant to hurt me. If I'm honest, what happened was more my fault than his. But I don't want you to worry about this. It's never gonna happen again...' She laughed. 'I think we must've stayed up the whole night talking.' She was quiet for a moment. When she spoke next, her voice was like ultra casual. 'Jinxy, I don't want you telling anyone at school about this, okay?'

'I won't.'

'Because it's our private business. You understand that?'

'Yes.'

'If anyone asks, I just tripped, coming down the stairs.'

My whole life till then she'd gone on about how important the truth was. 'Better a thief, than a liar,' she'd always said. Now she was actually instructing me to lie. I didn't know what to say to that and I think she was embarrassed, because she was quick to add:

'But I'm sure no one will ask you anything, so don't worry.'

As if that suddenly made everything okay.

'Guess what?'

Maybe she was speaking another language? I felt like I sometimes did in French, listening to tapes with French people talking on them, straining my ears for the odd word or two that I was actually able to understand, that put together with another word might make some sense of everything I was hearing. I was so confused it was beyond me to guess anything.

'What?'

My mother laughed again and, for a moment, she reminded me of Sam. It was the laugh the girls at school did sometimes when someone told them some guy they liked fancied them back, kind of surprised and giggly and blushing all in one.

'He's asked me to marry him.'

'Uh? Ow!' The comb seared the top of my left ear.

'That's your fault. You need to sit still.'

'That hurt!'

'I'll put some Vaseline on it, okay?'

'No it's not okay. It's not okay...'

'Come on, Jinx, you're being a baby. Don't you want your hair to look decent?'

'I was happy how it was before.'

'You want me to stop? I've only got a little bit left to do and we're done. Can I finish it?'

I nodded.

'Then stop crying. And sit still.'

I wiped my eyes as she continued. Other than the hot crackling of the comb it was silent. Then she asked, 'Well? What do you think?'

It was just too freaky. Even though he lived here, I still felt like I hardly knew him. And she'd only just taken him back last night. And that would mean he'd be with us for ever. This was my dad's house, but once they married it'd be like it was his. But she loved him and I knew it. She'd been happy since he'd been in her life and although she was asking my opinion like she genuinely wanted to know what I thought, I also knew she wanted me to *want* her to get married to him. She wanted me to say, *Yes, do it. What a great idea. We'll all be one big happy family*. I knew that.

'Isn't it a bit quick?'

'I'm not getting any younger. If we're gonna have our own kids, we need to get a move on.'

'Kids?' I felt dazed. Like she'd boxed me.

'You've always said you wanted a little brother or sister.'

It was true. I had. A million times. And the times I'd said it, I had truly meant it. Being an only child sucked. That was one of the things about Sam I was most jealous of. But this reality terrified me. And the words 'our own' made me feel sick, because I wasn't, was I? I didn't belong to them both. I was only hers. And a silly thought came into my mind, really childish but I couldn't push it away: do you love kids more if they belong to you and the man you're with? Is there enough love to go round? Or is there just a certain amount of it that gets divided up more ways so that somebody ends up with a smaller share?

'Have you finished?' I asked.

'I have. Shall I style it for you?'

'I'll do it myself.' I stood up.

'Well, what do you think?' she asked again.

I wanted to say, *I was here first!* Those were the words in my head that repeated themselves over and over like a stuck record, but it was too childish, too ridiculous to say.

'Do what you want. I don't care,' was the answer that came out instead. And before she could respond to that, I ran upstairs.

Sam was in a serious strop. She was vexed, her face was screwed up hard, and she did little more than grunt back when I said hello to her.

'What's up?' I asked.

She raised her hand in a Stop sign and shook her head. She was blushing badly. I didn't ask anything else, because I knew if she had said a word about whatever it was, she would have started to cry. If I was honest, her mood suited me. Though I couldn't get anything that had happened out of my head, I couldn't talk about it either. And it wasn't because of what my mum had said, the reason was even weirder: I was ashamed. I couldn't understand why I felt that way about what Berris had done to my mum, but I did. It was as if somehow what he'd done reflected on us, on my mum, as though in some way we deserved it or it was our fault, *her* fault. I felt embarrassed to hold my mother, with her outward-pointing toes, up to Sam's scrutiny. So even though I could have burst with the words stuck deep down inside me, I said nothing.

When we got to the bus stop, she carried on walking and I followed without question. She was doing some kind of funky walk, kind of like she was kicking imaginary leaves out of her way with every step and, at the same time, didn't really care if they were kicked out of the way or not. It took nearly fifteen minutes, till we were nearly at Dalston Junction Station, before her walk returned to normal and she finally spoke.

'So what happened to you yesterday?'

'I came on. I had really bad cramps so I stayed home.'

'Lucky you,' she said.

'*Bloody* lucky,' I threw back.

Though the lie came easily to my lips, I didn't look at her as I spoke because I was sure the fact I was lying my head off would be painted across my face. Desperate to get off the subject I asked, 'So did you speak to Donovan?'

'I've got better things to do than waste my breath on that renter,' she said. I took that to mean the talk hadn't gone well.

'Bet your mum bought you loads of stuff,' she said, but it came out sounding kind of resentful and for some reason made me feel embarrassed.

'Just some jeans,' I said.

'Nice.'

'I'da preferred it if she hadn't needed to suck up to me in the first place.'

'*My mum smacked me! And now she's bought me jeans,*' she whined. 'You're acting like you got the worse problems in the world, man. Grow up!'

She cut me deep and the rest of the way to school we trod in silence.

As if God had been listening and had not approved of my lie, halfway through double French I really *did* come on. With it came period pains so strong I felt nauseous. I hadn't packed any pads, so I had to go to the office to borrow one. I didn't want to go back to my lessons and I didn't want to go home. I returned to the office to ask for a couple of paracetamols and asked for permission to lie down in the sickroom till they took effect. The secretary gave me both.

The sickroom was the best place on earth for a person as wretched as I felt. Small and sterile, empty of everything, even medical supplies. It was like a broom cupboard painted white, with a small camp bed inside it, and on top of that a pillow, and on that a small, thin blanket folded neatly. Just the bed and a chair from one of the classrooms, and in the corner by the window, a small sink. No pictures on the walls, nothing to distract you from the objective of being there: getting well.

That morning, the dry, bare space felt like a sanctuary. I was angry with my mum, I was angry with Berris and now I was angry with Sam. For the first time in my life I felt completely alone. And old. Way older than sixteen and I wondered if my childhood was over, if the best and most carefree years of my life were already in the past, and how it had happened that out of the blue my life had become so full of confusion on every front.

At first break Sam came looking for me. She was shame-faced, like she knew she'd been well out of order. After a quick enquiry about how I was feeling, she flopped down on the chair with her arms folded across her stomach, and I swear she looked as unhappy as I felt. It was like the thing with my mum, like again I was still angry, but at the same time I knew she was sorry, and even if I'd wanted to, it was impossible to keep up a stand-offish front, because she looked so miserable.

'Are you gonna tell me what's up?' I asked.

'I found out Donovan's been two-timing me,' she said.

I tried to get my head around that. How he could be two-timing her when she hadn't told me she was going out with him in the first place and, secondly, I thought she wanted to blow him out, so what difference did it make if he went out with someone else?

'Oh,' I said. Even to my ears my response sounded a bit inadequate, so I quickly added, 'That's well weird.'

'All the while he's been going on like *yeah, baby, I love you*, and the whole time he's been saying exactly the same thing to some girl Paula, blacker than my bloody dad, with big old doo-doo plaits and buck teeth...'

I started laughing.

'It's not funny! He's been using me, all this time. Just using me,' she said and, *click!* just like that, it wasn't funny any more. I went from being a kid to understanding everything: that she'd felt more for him than she'd ever admitted to me; that like my mum, she was heartbroken, that she'd done It. With him.

'The bastard!' I said. Her face was getting redder and redder. I reached out and held her hand. She pulled it away.

'Don't or I'll start bawling my head off! Oh God...' – she stood up. 'Just thinking about it's making me feel sick.'

And she was. Sick. A combination of sobbing and vomiting that took us through the rest of the break. It was a lucky thing we were already in the sickroom with the sink right beside her, because if she'd had to make it to the girls' toilets, there would have been a trail of vomit through half the school all the way behind her. Although she'd come to see me because I was the one who wasn't well, I ended up having to get up and take care of her. Then, when we went to the office to tell them Sam had been sick and asked if she could stay in the sickroom as well, we ended up getting bawled out and were told we both had to get back to our classes, like we'd been lying and trying to skank our way out of our lessons.

Later, when we were supposed to be revising logarithms in maths with Mr Botha, between my stomach and my thoughts I couldn't concentrate on a word he was saying. I was lost, trying to get my head around relationships, how different they were in real life to Mills & Boons; how disappointing and seedy and unappealing. And I vowed I would never be like Sam or my mum, never cry over any man, never take their shit, never hand over the reins of my emotions, and I'd kill any man with my bare hands who ever tried to beat me. If what I was seeing was true love, I wanted no part of it. Any man who ever loved me would have to do it on my terms.

And they were: he would be light-skinned and sensitive and gentle and caring. He would be as good-looking as Superman himself, and like all the men in Mills & Boons, he would be mature. And experienced. Most of all, he would never hurt me or use me or do anything to make me cry. If he didn't match those criteria, he might as well forget it.

And for some very strange reason when I'd thought all that through, it was Lemon who came to my mind; Lemon, with his friendliness, his wide mouth, good looks and laughter.

The older, more sophisticated man.

And I shivered.

They'd been shopping. From the number of bags in the living room, it looked like they must have stopped and bought something from just about every single shop they'd passed on the way to the jewellers. My mother had mentioned marriage only this morning and by the afternoon, there it was.

The ring.

She'd also mentioned babies. Though he'd only been with us for two months, I wondered whether Sam was right, that any day now I'd be hearing the patter of little ostrich-shoed feet. Everything was moving too fast for comfort. It felt like I was playing catch-up.

She showed it to me.

Bling bling!

A white-gold band with a row of gems that twinkled and glittered every time she moved her hand, but no matter how hard they struggled to compete, they were overshadowed by her smile.

Berris said nothing. He sat on the edge of the settee, watching her watching him, the two of them playing games with their faces. It was like a whole language had evolved between them, one I could not speak or understand; whole statements made in the lift of an eyebrow, the puckering of lips, the cutting of eyes, the smiley mouths. Before, they'd had to go to bed to make me feel ignored. Now they were managing to achieve it even while I was in the same room.

He'd bought her a skirt, long and flowing, crinkled silk fit for a gypsy princess, and two pairs of shoes, pointy winklepickers I would have liked to have owned myself. She'd picked him out a bottle of aftershave because he only had like twenty bottles or so in his personal collection so far, and an LP by Roberta Flack, whose voice was strumming my pain with her fingers track by track as it played in the background.

And he'd bought her a real fur coat, a long one that fell from her shoulders to below her knees in thickest, darkest, sleekest brown. It was, without a doubt, the most luxurious and glamorous item of clothing she'd ever owned. It looked like mink, although he said it was just lame old cony fur from rabbits. Fur jackets were the cutting edge of cool and not only had I seen other women in them, but I'd longed for one myself. Hers was the first full-length one I'd come into close contact with, and it was by far the most beautiful coat I'd ever laid eyes on. In it, even I had to admit, she looked like a movie star, and she acted like one too, holding her hand in front of her mouth like a runway to launch the kisses she blew in his direction. All very Marilyn Monroe.

Finally, my surprise was brought out, in a green drawstring bag that identified it immediately. My instinct was to snatch it out of her hands, and it was only the fact that I remembered my age that stopped me.

'You bought me Dunlop plimsolls,' I said.

'Not me,' she said. '*We*.'

There was a time when if my mother had said *we* she'd have meant me and her. Now it was them. She was still a part of *we*; it was me who wasn't. *They* used to be other people, those who lived outside our home. Now *they* were inside; it was *me* and *them*.

In my view, it was a blatant case of curryfavouring. The fairy-tale king was becoming a fairy-tale father, so generous he was even prepared to treat the stepdaughter like his beloved own. I'd wanted those Dunlops for nearly a year, yet following fast on the back of the *we* comment, taking them out of the box made me feel ill.

'Try them on then,' she said, all excited. 'See if they fit.'

I toed a moccasin off one foot reluctantly and replaced it with a pristine white plimsoll.

'Perfect,' she said, though I wasn't sure if she was talking about the shoe or this fabulous new life of hers. She paused and waited, then quietly asked, 'What do you say?'

She'd hoped, I knew, that I'd have said it without the prompt. The words were there all right, clogging my throat, but I had to use the biggest force to get them out.

I glanced at him quickly and feigned a brief smile. 'Thank you,' I said.

I felt gutted, like everything in my life was wrong; somewhere I had taken the wrong turning and ended up lost. It was as if my mother's happiness was in direct proportion to my unhappiness, and any joy I had inside me was being sucked out to double her portion. I was running out of avenues in which to turn, and somehow she'd become oblivious to what I was going through.

Later that evening Lemon came round and, incredibly, I was as happy to see him as if he were *my* friend come to visit. He brought with him a bottle of Appleton's rum and some sweets in small white bags; a quarter of aniseed twist, a quarter of Tom Thumb pips, and a half-pound of pear drops, which he was particularly partial to; big ones encrusted in sugar, which cut the roof of your mouth if you got a bit impatient while you were sucking them.

I appreciated the sweets more than the plimsolls I'd so longed for. To me it was as if he'd actually been thinking of me and had made an effort to *not* make me feel left out, and it was ironic, because of everyone in the house at that moment, *he* was the outsider, the one I should have felt furthest from. Instead I felt closer to him than either Berris or my mum.

Lemon was the perfect house guest. He took no liberties. He didn't walk in with his bare hands swinging, dishing out demands. Not only did he not expect to be waited on, but he seemed to be on the lookout for chances to be useful. Why couldn't my mother have gone out with him instead? How much easier was he to get on with, to be around?

After dinner, he offered everyone drinks and it was Berris who told me to get up and give Lemon a hand, as though he was too busy to do it himself, and I was some sponger just sitting around scratching my backside. I went with Lemon to the kitchen where he made himself busy, collecting glasses, pouring liberal swigs into them and topping them up with the chaser.

'You just worry 'bout the ice,' he said with a smile, and I went to the freezer and pulled the tray out of the drawer. It was the gentleness in his voice and the smile that really did it to me.

I held it out to him and he took it from my hands, then asked, 'What's up?'

There is a moment when there is so much stored up inside it's like you could burst, when anger is the only way you can hold it together and just about keep it all in, when even the smallest act of kindness will push you over the edge, into the abyss of the bawlers. His question caught me in that moment. It was impossible to answer, way way way too vast. And everything that was wrong welled up in my throat and eyes thicker and faster the harder I tried to regain the smallest driest dregs of self-control. Suddenly all was lost and the tears spilled and I started to cry. Not any normal kind of crying, but the kind where once you start you need to cry up everything inside you, and nothing short of exhaustion or dehydration will allow you to stop.

He didn't say, *Hey, stop that.* Or, *Don't you worry, it'll all be okay.* Or, *What is it? Why are you crying like this?* He didn't even seem uncomfortable. The way he pulled me into his arms was natural. Like a father might have done, and he didn't need me to say a thing, as if my tears themselves were a language he understood and I didn't have to say a word.

I cried buckets. It was like I'd started out as a rain cloud and when the tears stopped, I'd become a fluffy white one hanging in a pale blue sky, basking in the light of Lemon, the sun. He released me then, went and pulled off a strip of kitchen roll and handed it to me to blow my nose. It was abrasive, scraping the rims of my nostrils like a scourer as I blew and blew, then wiped. Finally, testing my choked voice box, I uttered the word 'Nothing'. And he laughed.

'Well I'm glad it's nothing,' he said. 'If it was *something*, we woulda need to call out the coast guard.'

I sniffed and involuntarily smiled.

'That's better,' he said.

And to my surprise, I actually did feel better.

'Thank you.'

'S'no big deal. Most things, all they want is a little gentle handling.'

He put the last touches to the drinks and dropped in the ice cubes, then tidied up behind himself, putting everything back in its rightful place. He even wiped the cupboard sides down and when he'd finished, if you had come into the kitchen afterwards, you would never have known he'd been there at all. I don't know why, but that impressed me. Berris was meticulous about grooming himself. His shirts and trousers were ironed to perfection and at the point of his putting them on they were faultless, the seams brought to the zenith degree of sharp, which he admired in silence while running his clothes brush over them back and forth, removing microscopic specks that were invisible to every eye but his own. But on a domestic level, he seemed to expect – and my mother was happy to oblige – that everything was done for him. He sat like a god, entertaining himself with his music while she cooked, coming to the table to find his plate awaiting him, and when he was finished he just leaned back to let his food go down, and shortly after, as if by magic, she'd appear and take it away. Perhaps because Berris was the first man in my life – I couldn't really count my dad because I didn't remember enough about him – I'd come to think that maybe that was just how men were. But Lemon was different.

'Grab those,' he said when he was done.

He picked up two of the glasses on the table and I picked up the other two.

'The full one's yours,' he said. Then, 'You ready?'

I nodded and we carried the drinks back inside where we handed them out. I sat on the settee and watched Lemon settle himself on the floor in front of the stereo. A moment later, he was transformed into the music maestro.

Music was his passion. It was obvious. He selected records impeccably. He seemed to know exactly what tunes followed perfectly from the one before and his particular skill was setting and maintaining a mood and masterly judging the moment to change it.

He played and they danced.

Berris was a reasonable dancer. Not completely crap, but nothing special either. He had rhythm and he could hold a decent two-step, but nothing that made you want to watch him. On the other hand, my mum was wicked. She was compelling viewing anyway because of her looks, her high colour, her long legs and her perfectly rounded bum that made the back of her jackets fall into the soft curve of a duck's tail. She had been born to be beheld, and never was she more compelling to watch than when she danced.

She used Berris like he was a maypole, a baton in the hand of a marionette. She used him. In physics, we'd learned about malleability, the property of being able to take on different shapes, of being easy to form and reform, and that was what she was when she danced, malleable. As if her body was the sea, a wave, honey, the wind.

As I watched, I was suddenly overcome by jealousy. I wondered why so much had been given to some and others – specifically me – had been given so little. I discovered that I was even more jealous that she was dancing in front of Lemon, and he rocketed upward in my estimation of him when I realized he was purely focused on the music, glancing at them from time to time, but not with the hangdog open-mouthed adoration that Berris exhibited always. Lemon looked like he had even less interest in her than he had in watching Berris dance.

Four or five tracks later, she'd worn Berris out, and Lemon changed the tempo, brought it right down with Esther Phillips, 'Turn Around, Look at Me'. My mum and Berris melded into one intertwined dancing being, eyes closed, every part of the front of their bodies touching the other some-where; her head in the curve of his neck, his head folded downwards as if she were his favourite pillow, her arms around his waist, his hands flat against her hip and back, both of them moving so slowly, they were but a fraction of a movement removed from standing still completely.

I was so engrossed in watching them I hadn't seen Lemon get up, hadn't realized he'd come over till I felt him tugging me by the arm to stand and, when I did, he pulled me in his direction and we danced.

It was the first time I'd danced with a man. I'd danced with my mother many times, up close, eyes closed, but this was dif-ferent. Before, I hadn't thought about my body, hadn't been aware of it, had instead been consciously counting the beat in my head, like I was at a dance lesson aiming to learn something. With Lemon, however, I was aware of nothing but my body, the shape of it, the quality of every movement and how it would look to him; the jellying of my knees, the drumming of my heart, and the heat that blazed inside my body and intensified on the surface of my skin at every place I felt his slightest touch.

Most things just want a little gentle handling.

He held my waist lightly with one hand, scorching a hand-print there for ever, and his other held my free hand, pointing outwards as if we were dancing ballroom, with a respectable distance between our bodies of about a foot or so. His eyes were open, as were mine. It was the first time I'd seen him dance and it was obvious straightaway that he was good. Good enough to be the perfect partner to my mother. The knowledge made me feel even more ungainly.

All I kept thinking was, *This is it. The real thing. I'm danc-ing my first dance with an older, more sophisticated man and I'm in love, yes I am, oh my God, I love him.* At the same time I was stricken with embarrassment because I knew the way he was dancing with me was because he thought of me as a child when I wanted so badly for him to hold me close and treat me like a woman, to lay my head against his chest and have his arms wrapped around me tight for the rest of my life.

I died a thousand deaths wanting to watch him move, dreading he would catch me doing it, knowing he was watch-ing me and laughing, not out loud, just with his eyes, not at me but *with* me, because he was my older, more sophisti-cated man and the only person on earth who understood my suffering.

'Pull up, Mr DJ, come again,' Berris said and Lemon released me, lifted the needle back to the beginning of the track, turned the volume up a little more, then took me in his arms again, a fraction closer. Though it was a record we'd played many times before, for the first time, as we danced, I found myself listening to the lyrics.

There is someone watching your footsteps,
Turn around, look at me...

He looked through my eyes and into my soul. Though the words came from the stereo speakers, it felt like Lemon was talking to me aloud.

There is someone who really needs you,
Here's my heart, in my hand.
Turn around, look at me,
Understand, understand…

He knew me. Knew my anguish and how much I was hurting. A witch doctor of rhythm remedy and he was fixing me.

Look at someone who really loves you,
Turn around and look at me…

Releasing my waist he spun me around like a ballerina, with his other hand raised high above my head, holding my hand, then caught me in his arms at the end of the second revolution, closely enough against him for me to feel his heat, and my breath caught in my chest and I felt a rising dizziness that seemed connected from my head to my groin and I don't know how, but he knew it. I saw in his eyes that he did. And for one totally crazy mind-blowing moment, as our gazes locked, it was inevitable; he was going to kiss me then and there. My real-life Superman.

'This ain't no cradle-snatching business, Lem,' Berris said, and the moment disappeared like a balloon popping, vanishing into the space between us, as Lemon firstly stepped back, then let me go. 'You better remember you's a big old married man.'

I hadn't known he was married till then. The thought hadn't even crossed my mind. In my fantasy he'd been single, bowled over by the beauty he suspected lay beneath the darkness of my skin. Passionately in love with me. Ridiculous as it was, I felt like he'd cheated on me.

'Ease up Berris. They're just dancing,' my mum said.

Lemon walked back to the stereo and began flicking through the LPs leaned up against the stereo.

'You better go buy a guard dog,' Berris said to my mum and they both laughed. Lemon laughed too, without looking at me, but it was the kind of laugh you laugh when everyone's laughing at a joke and you don't want to make it seem like you're the only person without a sense of humour. I, on the other hand, wasn't laughing at all.

'I'm a big old married man,' he said drily. 'You don't need no guard dog on my account,' but it was me he looked at when he added that last bit and, like my mother, I went crashing from cloud nine straight on to the asphalt.

I'd made an utter fool of myself.

'I've got my biology revision to do,' I said lamely. 'I'm going up.' And as quickly as I could without running, I left the room.

Everything had been inside my head. He'd been laughing at me, not with me. I'd been a total idiot.

Upstairs, with a burning face, I relived the dance while a quiet bass vibrated softly from downstairs and I wondered what his wife was like, how old she was and whether he loved her. Though I felt like the world's biggest prat, it struck me that the difference in our ages was still smaller than the age gap between my mum and my dad, and that I was only a little younger than she had been when she'd gotten it together with Mr Jackson. Had she felt as I did now? Had she wondered what it felt like to be kissed by him? Had he known and laughed, then taken her? Was it possible that there had been nothing between us, that Lemon had felt nothing for me at all?

His wife had to be a witch, a fat old hag with a crooked nose and feet big as the susquatch, reeking of BO, her chin covered in coarse dark hair. Without a doubt, she was liquorice Mojo black, with pink rubber lips, alopecia and stinking breath. How could he not love me? How could he not?

And what evil, what merciless cruelty existed in the world for the only man I'd ever loved to be already married to another?

Forgotten was my earlier vow; how all would be on my terms, how I'd never let any man make a fool of me. I lay on my bed and sobbed and wept and crushed my hand against my breast in anguish. In the few hours since I'd sworn my vow of strength in love for ever, not only had I fallen head over heels, but I'd also managed to have my heart irreparably torn asunder into the bargain as well.

8

'When we growed up, back home, that was when things was all right and then things went all wrong. No matter how many times I go over it in my mind, that was where it started.

'First I give him food, then he become my friend. Then we was like twins, everywhere you see one, the other had to be close by. If it hadda been anywhere else on the planet but for that little island where everybody knowed everything about everyone living there, sure people woulda think we was brothers. Or poofters.

'We neither of us had brother nor sister to our name. In a way we was the only family the other one had, even thicker than blood. He scratched my back, I scratched his. The more we growed, the tighter we got, and everything was working out cool and dandy. Up to the day I meet Mavis.

'Up until then, we'd had women. Wasn't hard to have if you was a working man back home them times with little money in you pocket. I had my share. Shamed to say now was even a couple of times we had the same woman, wasn't nothing serious, you see. Was like lending you brother a wear of you shirt, allowing you spar a quick spin in you car, nothing serious. Them times in fact it was a laugh. Can't think of a single woman Berris really like if I'm honest, up until you mum. He was always talking 'bout how is money them looking for, man to take care of them jingbang, all of this kind of thing, on and on till it was like there wasn't a single woman on the island who had in her body but an honest drop. Every woman for some reason was out to trick. Not sure I believed it all, but didn't really matter anyhow because up until Mavis, I never found a woman that I felt something for above the waistband, you understand. When she come along, that was the first time I even come to consider what this word was all about that people call "love".

'Berris used to say that Mavis musta visit some obeah man; he musta give her some kinda potion that she slip ina my drink when me back turn, because he never see a man turn fool-fool so bad over one woman in him life. And I have to say it was true. Was the first time I ever wanted to spend time with anyone more than I wanted to spend time with him. Before that, even when we had women, they was with us, me and him. When Mavis come along, I suddenly find myself annoyed with Berris. It's like I only then realize how demanding he was. And he wasn't no more demanding of me than I was of him, but I'm just trying to tell you how it felt at that time to me.

'Mavis used to try persuade me to spend more time with him. He blamed her for not seeing me, but if it was down to her, chances are, me and her woulda never have a minute on our own. And I wanted her for my own. I didn't want to share her with Berris. Yes, it was selfish, but I was young and when you young, you know how it is; the thing you want most, be it a new pair of shoes, or to go to a particular rave, or to spend time with your new girlfriend, that thing is the most important thing in the world and nothing else even come close. So I didn't share. End up spending so much time just we two on our own, that was probably the reason she end up pregnant so fast.

'But the other thing was, I *knew* the man. He was already making comments, already telling me things he hear about goings-on with women who match Mavis description and the suchlike. He was jealous of her. Jealous bad. And he's always been the same, once he's in a temper, can't calm him down, have to act out the whole thing and pick up the pieces the next day or the day after, salvage what he can from the little rubble left over. I know two women got involved with Berris round them times and both of them, money or not, refused to sleep with Berris a second time. Truth is, I never want him anywhere near Mavis, because if he started in on his fuckry with her, how I was feeling then, I woulda had to kill him.

'Anyway, she end up pregnant, he say what him have to say 'bout the chances of the pickney being mine, etcetera, and I marry her. Think I was so vex with him I marry her to teach him a lesson; that from time to time it's necessary for a man to keep his mouth shut. Afterwards, when she find out what he was walking and telling people, she refuse to have him around her or in our yard. And I can't say as I blame her, because the man make up all manner of story and he tell two people: Who Ask and Who No Ask. Even so, I still kinda liked her, but because of what he said, it's like any trust we coulda had was killed stone dead. In a way, that helped things to work out okay. Me and Berris still used to hang round together all the time, work together, rave together, pick up the odd woman here and there and in truth, it was just like old times, 'cept I had the good luck after to come home when night done to find me dinner cook. Know this don't paint too decent a picture of me them times, but it's a true one and that's what I'm aiming at: the God's honest truth.

'Everything was fine and running to plan. Even after we leave Montserrat and come to England. He find a little place, then he keep an eye out for another little place for me near by. I get one foot through the door at Lesney's and I work till I open another door for him. Fine and dandy, everything was running smooth and sweet. Then one day, Berris met you mum.

'I thought I had it bad when I meet Mavis, but I tell you this: I know I said it before and I doubt you believe me, but I'll say it again anyway – Berris was in love. In a way, I think what he done and how he acted was kinda like what I did, except with him it was more, much much more. For example, I knew he was seeing someone because he was taking days off work, the odd one here and there, no reason for it, and afterwards telling me he done some old dryness with his time that I knew for sure was an out and out lie. Never said he had a woman, kept it, kept *her*, all to himself, but suddenly smiling all the while, always in deep thought, miss half of what

153

you had to say to him so you had to go over everything a second time; smartening hisself up – was always pretty smart anyhow, but went that one step further – and I knew what it was even without him telling me, but it pissed me off something that he never came outright and just said so. What was I gonna do if he told me? Sex her? The whole thing was a mockery! Didn't do a single thing but stir up some bad blood even before I come to meet her.

'Anyway, was out in a bar one Friday, on our way to some shebeens they used to hold down the top of Amhurst Road, and I speaking speaking speaking, repeating everything to him two, three, four times, and I finally lost it.

' "Me nah repeat myself again. If you can't keep you thoughts off the woman for long enough to hear what me a say, maybe you should go home to her," I said.

'I was vex, but Berris laugh like is joke me making with him.

' "Lemon," he said, "there is women and there is *women*. All these years, couldn't tell the difference. But I got me a *woman* now. Got me a woman to beat all women, I'm telling you."

' "I take it she just happen to be the one woman on the planet not after you money?" I said, and he laugh.

' "She no need my money. She own she own house, not a drop of mortgage on it, not a drop."

' "She must be a old bird then. Never thought you woulda prefer boiler fowl over spring chicken."

'He laugh again. "She's young enough. She married some old man died years back and leave her the house and a good pile of money."

' "And she fit?"

' "Lem," he said, "up until you see her, you don't even know the meaning of the word."

'I knew I was talking crazy, childish really, trying to find some kinda imperfection in this woman out of the blue he suddenly love, but I couldn't stop.

' "A widow, huh? So no virgin then. She have pickney?"

' "One. A girl child. Fifteen or sixteen or some such. Ain't met her yet."

' "Never figured you was one to go raising other men's kids," I said.

' "You know what, Lem, sometimes you have to weigh these things up. At the end of the day, I know what I'm getting straight up. The girl ain't mine and no one's trying to convince me to give up my money and freedom swearing she is. I know where I stand and that's all I want. I know for a fact there's 'nough man out there who would be glad for just one tiny bit of that peace of mind."

'It was the first time I really thought hard about the business with him and Mavis. Yeah, of course it come up in my head from time to time, but I never stopped before to dwell on it. Never really thought about why Berris acted like he done, but when he first met you mother, come like all of a sudden the foot was in the other shoe and I didn't like it one bit. In a way, how he done it all made me feel like he was cheating on me, which was rubbish of course, but that was how I felt. Then them little comments he made, always referring to Mavis and the boy, well they didn't help nothing at all.

'Truth be told, felt like I hated your mum long before I got a chance to meet her, and I know how childish that makes me sound but that was how, at the time, I did feel. Man, I dwell. Imagine all manner of corn on she foot, wig on top her dry head, hump on her back, the works.

'Even after she ask him to move in with her and he did, even up till then he never introduce me to her or nothing. I think he held it like a grudge, like he was saying "I can't visit your yard, you sure as hell ain't gonna visit mine." But really, it wasn't fair. He was the one who made hisself outcast from my yard. Whereas me, I never said nothing for him to go on them ways. Anyway, I bristle up, vex-face out, let him pay for his own pint down the boozer, little things really that shoulda been below me, but I stooped to them anyway just to make the point.

'And things was different. Before he moved in with her, I was round by his place most nights, even when we wasn't going nowhere, playing music and the such. After, was like a drought, me stuck indoors bored to tears, and Mavis so excited you woulda think it's honeymoon we on. I never willed the relationship no good, simple as that. I wanted it *not* to work, so things could go back to the way it was before. And above all, I *knew* the man, knew he could be charming, smiling all the while things was good, but that when things went wrong, he'd explode the way he always done. I knew all I had to do was be patient. My day would come. I wasn't happy but, still, I just settle back. All I had to do was bide my time.

'One day, I open up the front door and who should I see standing there, bawling, girl, bawling, but Berris?

' "Philemon! You have to help me, man!" he said.

'First thing come to my mind was the police must be after him. He musta rob a bank, thief something, kill someone. I even take a quick look up the road to see if my yard was under surveillance and the like as I quick time pull him inside and shut the door.

' "What happen, man? Talk no!"

'Even Mavis come a hurry out to look-see what a go on. Soon as she see is Berris, she push up she mouth and gone back upstairs.

' "Me mash everything up. Slap her down over some little stupidness. Knock her down like a man. I know she nah go want me back. Lemon, I blown it, blown things bad. I know I shoulda control myself. But I love her."

'When I realize is little domestic bring the man to pound the front door like hurricane warning, I had to laugh. And straight away him tense up, looking like he want to fight me too, only start to calm down when I explain to him me think he turn fugitive or something, though that wasn't the whole truth of it; I was happy. Knew things would sour after enough given time. They did and I have to say I wasn't just expecting it, I was glad.

'I beg him fix up himself, give him little brandy, and he explain to me what was in truth a little stupidness that he flare up for and smack her two smacks, etcetera. I wanted so bad to say to him that he had made a point of showing me this relationship was nothing to do with me, but I never could kick a man too tough when he was already down. So I did the only thing I could, I listened. And when he finished, he begged me to talk to her, to explain to her how sorry he was, 'cos he was sure if he went back to the house she woulda probably have him arrested, which was exactly what the man deserve.

'On and on, first begging then threatening, man recall every favour he ever done me in me whole life, if you listened too hard you woulda think the only thing he never done was born me. In the end couldn't take no more, had to say, "Yes. Yes I will go round and speak to her. Leave it with me. I will do what I can."

'When I clap eyes on her I couldn't believe it. Had to admit Berris was some kind of lucky bastard all right. Even with half her face looking like someone mash black grapes into it, she was beautiful. All that "beauty is in the eye of the beholder thing" seem like it never had the first bittta truth to it. Only person who coulda say she wasn't beautiful had to be a man walking with his shirt button inside out and his hands them holding on tight to a white stick. I wanted her for myself. Don't know which part of the house she woulda fit into on account of Mavis doing so good a job of using up every piece of free space I had, but I wanted her. Don't know which country I woulda have to go hide for Berris not to find me, still I wanted her. Made no sense to me. All I could think was maybe I was suffering some kind of male menopause, or mid-life crisis or some other kind of craziness you only even know exist because you can't sleep and end up watching foolishness on the TV in the early hours of the morning. I wanted her.

'I did my bit. Cuddle her and tell her how he never mean nothing, just a little temper, needing only a little understanding to change him, straighten him out. And it worked.

'After, when I speak to him, wasn't expecting no tough thanks, maybe just a "cool, man" or something, nothing big, you know what he turn round and said?

'"Pass back later for dinner, man. Make me teach you 'bout the kind of woman man supposed to marry."

'Serving up compliment with the uppercut as usual, and as usual it never miss the mark.

'"You better ask her," I said. "Make sure it's okay. She might not feel for no visitors, might not want to be bussing no big cooking tonight."

'"I make the rules where I live, and tonight I say we eat."

'I growed up with the man from youth, knew all the things he'd done in the past, and my mind shoulda know him for the type of person he was, but I never. Somehow, up till then, I think I believed what I told your mum, that he needed some love and some caring, that enough of that would bring about his change. But when he said that to me, *in his situation*, something in me changed for the worse.

'Feel shame to say this, poor Mavis probably still warm underground, but even though I feel shame, in my life I told so many lies, to her, to others, what a liar I was, so good I even manage to lie to myself, but no more. I vowed to myself I would try my hardest to be true, so I have to say this: I was like a dog.

'Man, I used to visit this house and watch Berris and you mum, mouth adrip, like watching another dog eat the wickedest, tastiest bone, watching the floor mostly, waiting for the odd scrap to drop, working out how to move on in without ending up in a serious brawl. I did some watching.

'Used to wonder what you mum see in him. Sure he was good-looking, but no more so than any other five-limbed man, no more so than me. Had fine clothes and shoes to kill, but not a drop of generous blood, not a single aim to please anyone other than himself. Used to see her beat up afterwards and wonder, what is it this man have over her? Often ask her, what is it about this man you love? Only conclusion I could come to was that having never really lived – you can't call what she did with your pops, old as he was, 'life' – having never had a young man naked in her bed, someone she could walk outta street with and see other women watching and wanting, downright made her lose every droppa common sense in her head.

'Even started to get vex with her when I see her all mash up. Couldn't say wipe your face and come with me to my house, not 'cos I couldn't get the words out. Fact is they was always so close to the tip of my mind and tongue it was more of an effort to keep them words in; that wasn't the problem. Problem was I know she woulda never do it. Was so wrapped round him, round his boot, his fist, his little finger, I know she woulda said no.

'At the time, I told myself I was frightened for her, frightened he would hurt her bad, but on its own, that wasn't the truth at all. I was jealous. Couldn't see why Berris, who I'm sure never even *liked* women, why him of all men should have a woman like that, what he'd done to *deserve* her.

'That was the first thing that went wrong, really. My feelings for her. No healthy place to put them, yet at the same time couldn't shake them off. That was the first thing. Second thing what went wrong was you. Don't know when and how I noticed you. Think it was the day we was dancing, definitely not before. Up till then, think I never really saw you, 'cos was only looking at the skin colour and thinking you was dark; I never noticed before then that you had her eyes and her mouth, that mouth always put me in mind of Brazil nuts, the shape, still does, and seemed like as soon as I noticed that, I noticed you was looking at me the way she was looking at him. Talk about from the pan to the fire. But I'm getting off the point.

'The thing is, bit by bit I was growing to hate Berris. Started out a little resentment, but it just kept getting bigger and bigger. Got to dwelling hard and carrying feelings. Thinking about ways to put him in his place came like my number one hobby after a while. That was bad enough, but it got to the point where that was the strongest of all the feelings I had, and I started saying things, small things at first, but things I knew would vex him. Started with the odd little comment in private: *Yeah man, she look good. Look like she happy to show it off too wearing skirts like that.* Soon, was doing what I told myself was only tick for tack pretty much every chance I got; slipping in a little honeyed uppercut myself, and leaving it with him to fester.

'Working on him alone was enough to cause middling upsets, can't deny it. Used to upset me something rotten to begin with that them upsets ended with your mother getting hurt. But after a while, think I musta started getting used to it, or maybe I somehow got a taste for it, don't know, but I took things to the next level, and that involved not just working him, but working her as well.

'So I started in on her. Small piece of advice, that was all it took. Mention to Berris that seems her blouses getting tighter and tighter. Mention to her that Berris always boasting to his friend them 'bout the way she dress, the way she look, especially in the chest department. If you have it flaunt it, etcetera. Little things aimed at causing minor controversy. Nothing big, mixing into every whopper some little truth to keep things real. Knew things were working because it got to the point where I was sure Berris couldn't sleep at night. Had him so wound up, looked like he pretty much wanted to fight the world and everyone in it one time.

'And even that was drowned out by all sense when they came home late that night, talking about what kind of wedding they was gonna be having and Berris boasting about how he was gonna be a daddy. I was rocking and acting like I was just listening to me music, but inside I was eaten up, eaten up bad. Woulda still been all right if he hadda stopped there, but Berris being the kinda man he was couldn't stop there, no. Had to go further, had to laugh and say the baby would finally give me a chance to be a real father, even if it was only a godfather.

' "But better a godfather than a jacket," he said, and I wanted so bad to knock him down but I just smiled. Smiled and thought what I could say to this man, living in his perfect kingdom, with the perfect wife and daughter and no doubt a young prince on the way, perfect as a tale out of a story-book. I went too far and I should've stop myself, but it's done now and that's that. Can't put the clock back, nor change anything that's gone before. Went too far the night of the engagement party as well. Was laughing to myself as I rubbed up on her 'cos I knew Berris, with his lead-foot self, woulda been stiff-up somewhere, vex-face watching. Knew I was playing with fire but convinced myself that everything I did then was justified, all was right and above all else, Berris deserved it.

'There's only three times I knowed for sure I'd gone too far. Every other time felt like I had the right to do what I did. Now I don't know. Feels like the one person who did deserve some comeuppance was me and I reckon I'm getting it now, reckon I'll probably be getting it till they put me under as well. Maybe after. Like to think I'll have done enough to join Mavis, but can't be sure of that, no matter how much I do. I'm sure wherever she is she don't have no worries, that the place she's landed is filled with light. That's the only place, the right place for someone like her who never did a living soul a scrap of harm.

'Whereas me now, I'm trying hard to build up the merits. Trouble is, the place I'm starting is so low, there's a whole heap I need to get hold of just to break even. I'm not even talking about getting ahead.

'But I'm getting off the point again, rambling like an old man. What I'm trying to say in this long, winding roundabout way is this: the space between love and hate is small, very,

very small indeed. And sometimes, a man can find hisself stuck there, like I did, and I tell you this much, you don't have room to move or turn, and it ain't exactly a menu, you don't have no choice at all. Your mother staying with Berris was love. What Berris did to her was love. And what I did to them both, I did 'cos of love.'

He had been making Guinness Punch, in the biggest pot I owned, an inherited one; mixing together the Guinness and whipped eggs, sugar, milk and Nutrament; grating in the cinnamon and nutmeg, lacing it heavily with rum. Methodically, using a tea towel folded in half, he crushed the ice placed inside it with a rolling pin. Slowly, he picked the pieces out and used them to fill the two glasses on the counter in front of him, then shook the remaining splinters off the tea towel into the sink.

'Told myself for years all was Berris' fault; everything I did was 'cos of him and the way he stay, but it wasn't true, I accept that now. Comes a time when a man has to do some reckoning with hisself, raise his hand for all he own and say, *Yep, I did that*. Never used to think like that before, but lately...Let's just say that's changed.'

'So what is it you're doing? Putting things right?'

'S'too late for that. Only thing I can try to do is put the record straight.'

'Well, you've done that.'

Why hadn't she told me?

'I'm not finished,' he said.

Using the ladle he poured his concoction into the glasses till they were full, then picked them both up and handed one to me. I took it, raised it to my lips and filled my mouth.

'I want you to forgive me,' he said.

Inside my mouth was a riot of flavour: savoury Guinness, creamy bitterness, aromatic spices, intense sweetness and, undercutting the lot, the alcohol's fiery warmth. My tongue moved about the mixture slowly. Wallowing.

I believed in honesty to a point and no further, as much honesty as a person needed to get to where and what they wanted, enough dishonesty to hide what should be kept private, like Family Business. Lemon was clearing up his past and his honesty was like bleach. He had been the Pied Piper, the music man. He'd set the tempo and they'd danced as he had mixed and changed the rhythm, then sat back to watch them pick up and follow the beat. And he wanted me to forgive him? I could not.

And yet, I had my own skeletons. Instead of decomposing over time, they'd fossilized. He had his share of responsibility and I had mine. He had manipulated and he had schemed, but I was the one who had murdered.

'I hardly know what use it is for me to say this, but I forgive you.'

He had been watching me, but he looked away then, down to his own glass, which he raised quickly in cheers before knocking it back.

'This is good,' I said.

'Thanks.' His voice was thick with feeling.

It was too much. Everything. I put down my glass and covered my face with my hands and began to cry. Inside me raged the anger of the betrayed, the shock of the double-crossed. Lemon came over to where I sat, pulled me into his arms and, holding me close, rubbing my hair, asked, 'What?'

The words were so big I could hardly get them out, but I pushed.

'How come she never told *me* she was pregnant?'

9

Over the next couple of months I came to feel like I'd been duped. She felt it too, my mum, though she did her best to try and style it out like everything happening was normal, and her and Berris were just fine and hunky-dory. But that man had tricked us good and proper, and I knew it.

Those first few months he'd lived with us had all been some huge kind of act. Somehow, he'd kept all his aggression locked up tight where my mum wouldn't spot it, concentrated on worming his way in so tight that now, not even a crowbar could shift him. Or maybe it was her taking him back that did it. Maybe after that first incident he thought that whatever he did she would always take him back and forgive him. Or maybe he'd just gotten the taste for it back, and I mean *back*. Him vexed, him angry, whatever it was inside him that made him want to hurt others, hurt her, that was his genuine character, how he was when he was relaxed, how he looked when you caught him in unguarded moments; *that* and not what we had seen at first was his true nature and

I just knew, I don't know how, but deep down inside, I knew he'd done this before to other women, that after months of pretending to be something and someone else, that after the first time, he'd gotten the taste back. And I was terrified.

While he was at work she was home all day. As far as I could make out, she was at home doing nothing except thinking about him: shopping for him, cooking for him, moving the furniture around into different positions she thought would appeal to him; that was pretty much it. But to listen to him in his rages you'd think she'd been out on the prowl constantly for the attentions of other men, that she was thinking of nothing else but attracting them, that her head was filled from morning till night with being with them, doing things with them. And Berris was obsessed with catching her at it.

Sometimes he'd pop home unexpectedly in the middle of the day, or he'd get in from work hours before he'd told her his shift was ending, or he'd return home shortly after leaving for work saying he'd made a mistake and was actually off work that day. These things he appeared to me to do with the express intention of catching her red-handed.

Only the day before he'd given her a rocketing slap. In front of me. Because his dinner wasn't ready when he came in and she was wearing fishnet stockings, and she couldn't explain quickly enough to his satisfaction why she was wearing them *and* was late cooking. I couldn't even fathom a connection between the two things, they were that unrelated in my mind, but for that he'd split her lip. Though it was the first time he'd done it in front of me, it wasn't the first time he'd busted her mouth.

It was puffed and swollen the evening he gave her the black suede three-quarter-length coat, with a sheen like richest velvet and a black leather trim that might have been hand-stitched it was so delicate and divine. And her hip where he'd kicked her was livid with bruising that made it painful for her to stand when she first tried on the sheepskin: camel-coloured, with a deep-pile chocolate lining that pushed its way out and over into a dense plush collar that was soft and warm and luxurious. And he'd had to help her to put on the yellow leather box jacket, patiently standing behind her and holding the right side low enough for her to get her hand into the sleeve, because her mashed shoulder prevented her raising her arm, or even moving it much. Up until then I'd never even imagined you could get leather in colours like that: a pale yellow with the slightest tinge of green in it that reminded me of a fiery French mustard. Every one of those coats was so beautiful they made a person ache just to look at them. Truly ache.

And the tears, the ones that had set us up the first time, the ones that had seemed so much like the real McCoy, that had made me feel sympathy when I should have felt fury, made her take him back when she should have banished him for ever – those crocodile tears were history. He no longer stormed out, or bawled, or looked ashamed or even sheepish when he did what he did, or when he gave her the coats after-wards. He would watch her as she struggled to smile despite the pain, watch her twirling and spinning inside them, as if every gift she'd ever been given in her life had followed on the tail of a roasting and she expected no different, and his own face would be set with a smile that was smug and satisfied; his eyes when they met mine were challenging, daring me to say a word.

And Lemon came and spoke to her every time. With Berris and me she acted like everything was cool, nothing was going on that was ugly or crazy or way too wild for any mortal being to understand. For us she continued churning out those yummy platters of dishes marinated overnight and slow-cooked over low heat for hours. But alone with Lemon she cried. After one of them had given me food or drink or sweets and banished me to my bedroom so they could get on with their talk without having to worry about the big ears of little donkeys. But I could always tell when she had been crying because she was like Sam. Maybe all people with high colour were like that when they cried; all red eyes and noses and blotchiness that made it impossible to pretend that they'd been doing anything else. In private with Lemon she cried, and sometimes just knowing that was enough to make me cry as well.

But the evening of the day after the slap he gave her in front of me, I crept back downstairs and listened. I needed answers too. It felt like Berris was going further every time. He'd been hurting her in private. Now he'd progressed to doing it in front of me. What was left? Would he start knocking her down in public? *Then* what? I was scared because I couldn't work out just where all of this was going to end. So I crept halfway back down the staircase in the darkness, sat on a step, pressed my face between the spindles of the banister, and listened to them.

She sounded like a poor swimmer trying to speak while doing doggy paddle, talking too quickly, spluttering her words in gasps between wet breaths.

'Tell me, tell me what I'm doing wrong,' she said. As though what was happening was her fault, not his. As though maybe Berris was the victim.

'It's not you, it's him,' Lemon answered. 'The way he is. Never had nobody to trust before and it takes time to learn that. You gotta give him time.'

'*If* he comes back...'

'He'll be back.'

'I don't know if I can take it.'

'But you love him?'

'Yes.'

'Then you don't have no choice,' he said, and for a while all I heard was her crying.

'I'm so scared,' she said finally.

'I know.'

'Of being alone.'

There was a rustling noise, then I heard her blow her nose. It was his turn to be silent. I thought that, like me, he must have been digesting her fear of Berris *not* coming back, when what any sensible person should fear most was that he *would*. But when he answered, I realized he must have been thinking about something completely different.

'Look at you. How could a woman like you be afraid of being alone? You think Berris is the only man alive who can see?'

'But I was. For years. More than ten years. I can't go back to that.'

It felt funny hearing her describe her life with me as though I wasn't in it. Funny hiding outside on the stairs, unseen, hearing her say that.

'Because you love him?'

'Yes.' It was quiet for a bit. Then, 'He's all I have. I can't go back to how it was before, being a single mum again, every decision mine, night after night with no company, just me on my own with the ticking clock. I'm not one of those women who don't want to cook, who don't want to listen. He tells me to do something and it's done. But *this*? I can't understand why it's happening. Why is he doing it? Why?'

When Lemon spoke, his voice was so low it was a strain for me to hear it. 'Look at you with you crying and you bawling and you moaning and complaining. You think Berris want a woman to walk over? The man don't need no doormat. You want respect you gotta earn it. Show him your own mind. Let him see you can do for youself. Let him know you's not some kinda bups he's dealing with.'

She laughed, loud and disbelieving. 'I think he'd probably kill me.'

'Remember I known Berris his whole life. Don't need no private investigator to tell me what he want. I heard it myself, straight from the horse's mouth.'

'Berris told you this himself?'

'Would I lie?'

'And you really think it'd work?' For the first time during their discussion there was hope in her voice.

'I *know* it will,' he said.

This time when she laughed it sounded like a proper laugh. 'Look at me. I'm a mess. I think I need a cup of tea,' she said.

'Let me get it.'

I stood up as the living-room door opened and Lemon stepped out into the hallway. He looked surprised to see me. I was styling it for dear life, like no way had I been earwigging, just coming down the stairs naturally, and he looked kind of puzzled, like he was trying to see through my act.

'Hi,' I said.

'I'm making hot drinks. You want one?' he asked.

'Please.'

On his level now, I paused outside the living-room door.

'Give you mum a few minutes,' he said. 'Come and keep me company.'

In the kitchen, I sat at the table and watched him. The male equivalent of my mum. Everything he did was so graceful; the way he stood, the stretch of his legs as he reached into the cupboards above the sink, the line of his arm as he lifted the kettle, the way they folded across his chest as he leaned against the sink, watching me and waiting for the water to boil. Again, that crazy certainty; he knew everything I felt without me saying a single word. Still, though, I said them, the words uppermost in my mind, the ones that had kept me awake the night before.

'He's going to kill her.'

'No,' he said, 'he's teaching her a lesson.'

'What lesson?'

'To respect him. It's how we all came up: respect the teacher otherwise you get you arse cut, respect you grandmother or you aunty or you mother otherwise you get you arse cut; respect you man...It was a lesson in respect.'

In the silence he put his hand against the kettle, felt its clammy coldness and, realizing his mistake, pressed the button, turning it on. I didn't know what to say to that. It felt like 'respect' was the wrong word but I didn't know what the right word was.

'Is she gonna be okay?' I asked.

'Depends what you mean by okay,' he said. 'Nothing's broke. Her face will heal.'

'This time. But what about next time?'

'It'll be fine,' he said after a long pause. I waited for him to elaborate but he didn't. He concentrated on the cups, putting the tea bags in, pouring the water, stirring. Finally he asked, 'Sugar?'

'Two,' I answered.

He was trying to change the subject, treating me like a child, like it was that easy to make me forget, to get me focused on sugar and sweeties instead of murder.

'How do you know?'

He sighed and stopped stirring. 'Jinx, Berris is a very particular man and he likes things a very particular way. You mum just need to mind when he speak. If she can do that, she won't have no problems with him.'

He had just said the opposite of what I'd heard him saying to her and I was shocked. I wanted to say something, but didn't know how to without exposing the fact that I'd been hiding on the stairs listening to them. Why would he have said such different things to the two of us? When I thought it through, knowing what I did about the type of person Berris was, what he'd told *me* made more sense. And almost immediately, it came to me. I knew why he'd lied to her and I wondered how I'd missed it before. He liked them being together no more than I did. If my mum followed his advice it would make things worse, not better, possibly even break them up for good. For a second, looking at Lemon was like seeing my reflection. He and I were one and the same and we wanted the same thing. I felt that unidentifiable stirring in my lower belly again. He must have been such a sweet boy when he was young. He was, even for an old guy, one of the most attractive men I'd ever seen.

He handed me my cup of tea. Embarrassed, I took it, then looked away.

'Thanks,' I said.

'Any time.'

I missed Sam badly. I should have told her about what was going on at home from the beginning, but I hadn't and it was like the more things that happened, the further I kept getting from the possibility, as if my whole life was a dark, dirty secret that was getting harder to explain the longer I left it, and at the same time all I could think about was discussing it with her.

I needed her.

I needed someone to talk to so bad at times it felt like the pressure of keeping everything inside would drive me crazy. But she'd stopped coming to school. She'd been off for nearly three weeks straight, even though we were supposed to be doing our O levels in two months' time. I'd been to her house but I didn't get past the front doorstep. Mrs Adebayo had acted so weird I hadn't dared go back; so weird that only some kind of enormous shock could have made me go back, something that freaked me out to the max. And that's exactly what I got.

For the three weeks Sam had been off, things had chugged along predictably at school. Then one morning, during registration, when our form tutor called the register, he missed off her name.

The class register was like a poem we'd been memorizing for five years, with the odd change here and there, but otherwise pretty much the same, and during that time Sam's had always been the first name called. From day one. I was so accustomed to the rhythm of the register that Mr Botha had made his way through the following five names before I even realized it was being called.

'Sir, you forgot Sam Adebayo,' I said.

Mr Botha paused between names and looked at me. You were supposed to put your hand up if you wanted to speak, and I hadn't.

'Samantha is no longer a pupil here,' he said. 'I'm surprised you of all people didn't know that.'

I felt like I could hardly breathe with the hammering inside my chest. He resumed his call and I sat and tried to think of a single spin I could put on what he'd said that would make those words mean something else. At break time I went to the office, but the secretaries wouldn't give me any more information than I already had. Sam was no longer a pupil.

Why wouldn't she be coming back? What was going on? I stayed through physics, but as soon as the bell went for lunch I left. The only thing I could think about was going to see her, going to see and speak to the only friend I'd had for the last five years.

By the time I reached Pembury Estate it was a little after one. All the way there I hoped the rest of Sam's family would be at school and work, because if her mum answered the door I might as well forget it. Outside their flat I rang the doorbell, then knocked the letter box, then rapped on the pane of glass in the front door first with my finger, then my key, but there was no answer. No one was in. She was my best friend and I would never see her again. My eyes smarted from the sheer unfairness of that on top of everything else going on in my life.

Then, for a split second, I thought I saw someone or a shadow shift past the kitchen window and I threw myself at the door, hammering and pounding away and calling her name. I felt reckless with desperation. I didn't care any more if it was Mrs Adebayo inside, I just needed to see someone, anyone who could explain to me what was going on. There was someone in the house and if I had to pound all day I would. I swore I would not stop till the front door opened. And it finally did. What felt like ages later. And there stood Sam.

'Oh my God! Where have you been?' I asked her.

I wanted to hug her, but her body language was kind of hard to interpret. She moved back as though she knew the instinct was in my head, stepped back out of reach, and she shrugged.

'I've been sick.'

'For so long?' I asked, studying her. The amount of time she'd been off I would have expected her to look half dead or something, but she didn't. She looked normal. A bit pale, but that could have been the shapeless black jumper she wore. It hung on her like a baggy dress. Dark colours always made her look a bit anaemic.

'Yeah,' was all she answered.

'Where's everyone?'

'My dad's gone down the market. You can't stay long. If he catches you here I'll be in even more trouble.'

'You don't look sick.'

She shrugged again. 'You coming in?'

I stepped into the hallway and waited while she shut the door behind me. She passed me and I followed her into the living room. There I found a state of chaos. There were towels and dresses and T-shirts, masses of clothing and underwear strewn about the settee, and in and around a couple of suit-cases that were opened and being packed on the floor.

Some of the stuff was obviously newly bought, but the older stuff I recognized as Sam's. When I met her eyes, my own were questioning.

'They're sending me to Ghana,' she said with a slow blush rising.

I was terrified. 'For a holiday?'

She shook her head. 'For good.'

'But why?'

'Guess.' But she didn't sound like she had the slightest interest in playing games and I didn't either. It was too serious, too final for jokes.

'I can't.'

'I'm pregnant,' she said.

'Oh my God…Who for?'

She rolled her eyes in exasperation. 'Donovan, innit.'

'Does he know?'

'Yep. Does he care? Nope.'

'When's it due?'

'Six months. S'what the doctor reckons.'

'But what about your O levels?'

'School's saying I can't sit them. I'll be showing by then.' Her face was beetroot now. 'Please don't tell anyone,' she said, and the first tears fell.

'I won't,' I answered and, moving forward, finally hugged her.

'Swear on your mother's life.'

'I swear.'

'I don't want everyone laughing at me.'

'No one's gonna laugh.'

She pulled away from me. Went and yanked a tissue from a box on the table, flicked it out then carefully folded it in half. 'Why not? I've been so stupid.' She blew her nose.

'You don't have to go. You could run away.'

'And go where?' she asked in a voice that was completely flat. 'It's not just me any more.' Years she'd been talking about leaving home, getting her own place, doing her own thing, as soon as our exams were over. All that bravado had gone. It was like she had no more choices now. Like all options had been brought down to this one unimaginable one. What had her parents done to her to get her to this point? How had they broken her? Could this really be the last time I'd ever see her? I wondered why I wasn't crying myself.

'You better go. Before my dad gets back.'

'I don't want you to go,' I said, and as if someone had pulled the chain, my own eyes filled.

'Can you imagine me as a mum?' she asked.

I nodded. 'You'll be the best.'

'I'll write to you,' she said. 'Send you pictures and that.'

'Okay.'

'Promise me, Jay, you won't make the mistake I did. If you end up with a black guy, get a costume. My mum told me enough times. I wish I'd listened.'

'Okay.'

'If you don't, you'll end up wasted. Like me.'

'You're not wasted.'

'Promise me,' she said.

Even if Sam had worn a collection of costumes to bed every single night of her life, it wouldn't have stopped her getting pregnant, because she hadn't gotten pregnant in the night-time lying in her own bed, but in the daytime over the garages under Nightingale Estate. She was such a drama queen. Would there be anyone in Ghana to love that about her? 'I promise,' I said.

'He could be back any minute. You have to go.'

But I threw my arms around her instead and hugged her for the last time. I didn't want her to leave me on my own. She was the last person I had left. In the end it was her who untangled me and literally pushed me out the front door.

It was too late to go back to school and too early to go home without a thousand questions, so I walked up to the high street, went into the library, found a quiet corner to hide in and sat there for hours. Everyone I cared for was vanishing before my eyes, moving out of touching distance, leaving me behind to face the emptiness alone. I felt like I'd been boxed into a tight place with too little air to breathe and I didn't know just how I was supposed to make it through the rest of my life.

They were dancing to Randy Crawford when I came in. High day in broad daylight, and the two of them had their arms wrapped around each other, dancing in the middle of the living-room floor, locked away in their own private world, oblivious to everything. Neither of them heard me enter the room. More spookily, they didn't even sense me as I stood watching them. It felt like it wasn't just my life and the people in it that were vanishing, it was my very person, like if something didn't happen soon, I would cease to exist.

She was wearing the red high-heeled clogs again and a black coat I had never seen before that fitted her so close it was like it had been tailor-made. It goes without saying it was beautiful: leather, falling over her body almost to the ground, with a red satin lining that shocked every time the split at the back shifted to reveal it. When the track ended, it was Berris who opened his eyes and saw me standing inside the doorway. He stiffened and his smile faltered. He tapped her on the back with his fingers, lightly. Slowly, she opened her eyes and, as the haze lifted, finally realized I was there.

She smiled and winced and instinctively her finger went up to her face, touching the bruised lip and checking her finger for signs her mouth had begun to bleed. Then she remembered Berris and glanced at him quickly, curling the finger along with the others into her palm, giving him a small smile and touching him with that same hand as if to say, *It's okay, honey, it's healing.* She whirled away from him, coming to a sultry pose in front of me even though that coat required nothing whatsoever from her to look good.

'Do you like it?' she asked. 'Berris bought it for me. Isn't it gorgeous?'

'It's wicked,' I answered, and it was. 'Hi,' I said to Berris.

When he smiled at me his eyes were mocking, but swiftly, they returned to her, because nothing else of importance existed for him anywhere.

'What's for dinner?' I asked.

'I'm taking you mother out,' Berris answered, looking at her as if she might be one of the items on the menu. He asked, 'Did you tell her?'

My mother looked a bit embarrassed. 'She knows we're getting married,' she answered.

'I'm talking 'bout the party,' he said.

Her colour rose a fraction higher. 'Did I say we were having a party?' she asked, as though she couldn't quite remember, when we both knew blatantly she hadn't.

'No.'

'For the engagement,' Berris said.

'Oh.'

'On Saturday. You can invite as many of your friends as you want,' she added.

I couldn't think of a response to that. 'What time you going out?'

'About eight. Lemon's coming round to babysit –'

'I'm not a baby.'

'I know, I know. He's just gonna be here till we get back, just in case...,' she said.

'Of what?'

'Come on, Jinxy, don't be difficult.'

'I'm sixteen. Stop treating me like a kid.'

'I've fried you some chicken and plantain,' she said too fast. 'And some coleslaw and potato salad and rice. I know you've got revision and stuff to do, I just didn't want you to be here till late on your own. That's all.'

'Fine,' I said. Then Berris took hold of her hand and pulled her into his body and they picked up the beat of 'Secret Combination' first with their feet, then their hips and thighs, then her head was against his chest, and their eyes closed.

When they left hours later, the top of the house smelt like a whirlwind had passed through a cosmetics factory: Skin so Soft and cocoa butter and Dax and hairspray and Brut and Soft & Gentle and Chanel No. 5, a dense cloud so cloying it threatened to suffocate those of us who remained behind.

I stayed in my room. In the pre-Berris era, my mother would have sought me out and given me a kiss before she left. That night, however, she remembered me only as an afterthought on her way down the stairs, chuckling at something Berris had said, shouting goodbye through a throat full of laughter. I doubt she even realized I hadn't answered, like she was nowhere near noticing how miserable my life was, how much I needed someone to be there for me and how wretched I was that there wasn't anyone.

Though I hadn't yet seen him or said hello, I knew Lemon was downstairs. I could hear the low music playing. I didn't care if it came across as rudeness; he could go hang. I was sick to death of concerning myself with other people when it was clear that no one was concerning themselves with me.

For a couple of hours I sifted through textbooks and notes, trying to revise, taking nothing in whatsoever. She'd been with me, Sam, in all of these lessons, and everything I touched reminded me of her, of notes we'd passed and jokes we'd cracked, and the billion things we hadn't yet done that we would never have the chance to do now.

It was ultimately hunger that drove me out of my room and downstairs to where the curry-favour banquet was that my mother had prepared, all of it stuff I liked. I virtually tiptoed down the stairs, stepping in time to the bassline of 'I Shot the Sheriff', hoping I wouldn't encounter Lemon, then for some weird reason when I didn't, feeling disappointed. I paused outside the living-room door, holding my breath, spying on him through the crack on the hinge side. He was lying on the floor with a cushion under his head. His arms were folded over his chest, his legs crossed at the ankles. Eyes closed. His fingers and his feet danced.

It was the first time I'd had a chance to study him unobserved. For a moment, I forgot my stomach and just looked. He wore a pale cream cotton shirt, the wrists folded over several times loosely. His forearms were hairy, or maybe they seemed hairier than they really were because the hair on them was thick and dark and contrasted hard against the paleness of his skin, which was maybe even slightly lighter than my mum's.

The older, more sophisticated man.

He wore navy slacks that fit him snugly and it was easy to imagine him naked, so perfectly sculpted were his legs inside them. I bet they were covered in hair too, like his arms were. His trousers were especially tight and raised high over his wood and I wondered whether it was just his wood that filled out that part, or was it hair as well, a thick Michael Jackson Afro of pubic hair? It was so tantalizing and at the same time so ridiculous that I laughed out loud.

His eyes opened.

My dash to the kitchen was clumping and clumsy and, to style it out, I was doubly noisy, banging the cupboard doors and crashing my plate on to the table, rustling through the containers in the fridge, desperately trying to compose myself, willing my breath back to normal. When I closed the fridge door and straightened up, he was standing just inside the doorway, watching me like he was trying not to laugh. The bowl of coleslaw in my hands felt heavy. I put it down on the table, beside my plate.

'Thought it was some kinda stampede going on in here,' he said.

'I'm just getting something to eat 'cos I haven't had my dinner yet,' I said, praying that the blush I felt could not be seen, while at the same time positive it was just blatant. My hands were shaking as I peeled the clingfilm from the bowl. I couldn't meet his eyes.

'You need help?'

I shook my head.

'You sure?'

I nodded.

'You think the fridge door likely to ever open again?'

'Funny!' It was a feisty answer for me, but instead of making me feel embarrassed, it made me feel bolder. Not bold enough to look at him, but my hands were steadier as I forked out some coleslaw on to my plate and smoothed the clingfilm back into place.

'I'll sort myself out,' he said, as though I'd offered to dish up food for him as well.

'Right,' I answered, putting the bowl back into the fridge and making a show of closing it in slow silence.

'You sure there's nothing you want?' he asked, and it felt as though his voice had plucked a string. Low down in my belly, even lower, something went *twang*. I couldn't look up. I couldn't move. My legs felt like jelly beneath me and I didn't trust them enough to even shift my weight. I nodded.

'I'll be inside if you change you mind,' he said and then he was gone.

I was too wound up to eat. Too wound up to even know what it was that I wanted to do instead. I put a dish over my plate and put the whole thing in the fridge. I went back upstairs, ran a bath and sat in it. It was Lemon's body I thought about lying there in the warm water, feeling my own body, so familiar and at the same time so different, sensitized in new places to the heat, the lapping, touch.

Out, I dried myself off, creamed my skin and put on deodorant and a clean pair of knickers. Wrapped in a towel, I padded back to my room and put on a dressing gown. I thought it might cheer me up putting on a little make-up, that looking good on the outside might make me feel good on the inside. In my mum's room, sitting in front of the mirror, I put on mascara and blusher, then carefully, with hands that were insufficiently steady, a dark plum lipstick. I examined my reflection, trying to decide whether I looked sexy or silly, then because I truly couldn't make my mind up, I wiped it all off. I reapplied the mascara in the hopes of making my lashes look fuller and my frog eyes smaller. I didn't know if that worked either, but I left it anyway.

I felt brazen. I was a little girl playing at being a grown woman and the thought that Lemon could have even the slightest interest in me was ridiculous. Not only was he married but I knew without ever having set eyes on her that his wife was gorgeous, like my mother, light-skinned and graceful, with long coolie hair and a deep husky laugh, and him finding me sexy was as likely as any man preferring corned beef to T-bone steak. I abandoned the whole scenario in my mind, the Mills & Boon fantasy, images of Lois Lane and Superman. I realized I was hungry again and, following the sound of music, went back downstairs.

When I walked into the kitchen he was sitting there eating, and when he looked up at me I froze and he stopped chewing. I no longer felt brazen, I felt naked under his eyes, my Superman. Did he have X-ray vision? Could he see through my dressing gown? Did he know how little I wore beneath it? I fought to keep on moving, to look natural. My legs were trembling so bad, I wondered if I was going to fall over in front of him. If that happened, he'd have to call an ambulance because I wouldn't be getting back up. I would be too shamed. I'd have to pretend to be unconscious. If my legs buckled and I ended up on the floor, I'd actually prefer it if he thought I was dead.

'I left you plate in the fridge,' Lemon said, and his voice sounded different, but I couldn't be sure if it was really his voice that was different or whether the blood pounding in my ears just made it sound different to me. I felt a stirring low inside my stomach, kind of like a rumble but different, more tense. He was eating a piece of plantain, sliced and fried. The oil on his lips made them shiny and, as I watched, he licked them.

'I'm not hungry,' I said, and dragged my eyes upward to focus on his. He put the cutlery down.

'Don't look at me like that,' he said, and I knew it wasn't the blood in my ears then, that his voice really was choked, because he cleared his throat.

I didn't know what to say, how exactly you did this kind of thing. I wanted to say 'I love you' but if I said it and he laughed I would die. More than anything, I wanted him to tell me he loved me. But I couldn't ask that, the words wouldn't come, so I just said, 'Please.'

He stood up and walked over to me, standing close, reached out his hand and oh so gently slowly touched my face, my mouth, with a fingertip, tracing its shape, watching himself as he did it. I wanted more than his finger there, I wanted his mouth to crush down hard on mine, my older, more sophisticated man, I wanted his tongue inside my mouth, to breathe him in and swallow him. I wanted him to possess me. I said it again, 'Please.'

He said what I already knew in my heart. 'You's just a child.'

Even though I knew it was the truth, it was like a physical blow, a super-punch, winding me. All I wanted was someone to love only me, not even for ever, just for a moment, just to know how it felt to be desired, to be the only person wanted by another human being, and he was the only person left to ask and he'd said no. I started to cry. He'd called me a child and it was beyond me to do anything more than act like one. The tears made my humiliation complete. When he tried to pull me into his arms, it was too late. I pushed him away and I ran.

He chased me, calling my name, shouting *Wait!* but I couldn't stop because I was running away from everything in my life, not just him. On reaching my room, I burst through the door and tried to shut it behind me, but he was already too close, half his body already through, and he flung it open and took me in his arms, kissing me, small pecks, over and over, and when he finally kissed me on the lips I realized

I had never lived, that I'd never known anything, that up until that moment I truly had been a youth, that what I'd been doing with oranges had been child's play.

His mouth possessed me.

His hands, hot hands, found their way inside my dressing gown and he groaned to find my skin bare, like a man lost, his palms gliding over my nakedness, branding trails that in the darkness would have glowed like kryptonite.

There was a hollow near the base of my neck, like the eye of a tornado, which tried to burst through my skin when his teeth scorched that spot and I gasped. Pulling the gown apart his mouth found a place to feed, and as he sucked I thought my legs would finally give, felt a hardness where before only softness had existed, every nerve in my body concentrated in the single nipple parrying his thrusting tongue.

And slowly, oh so slowly, like he didn't want to scare me, his hand made circles on my stomach, moving lower and lower till he touched me there, through my knickers, where he pressed his fingers and, as if he'd flicked a switch, an electric current surged upwards through me, escaping my mouth in the shape of a moan.

'You're beautiful,' he whispered. 'Beautiful.' Then he stopped and sank to his knees and pulled my underwear down. I lifted a single shaking leg to free them, and they fell around the other like an ankle bracelet. He shifted my feet so my legs were more apart, then his fingers touched me there, doing more parting of their own, and then his mouth.

The only thing that kept me standing was the door against my back and I braced myself against it as my heart moved from my pounding chest to the part of me he licked like a lollipop, till it throbbed as if it would burst. Then he stood and undid his belt, and his button, and his zip, and pulled his clothing down and his privates touched my privates then he was in me, filling me, then stuck.

'Oh my God!' he groaned. 'Oh my God!'

He pushed again and something gave and I knew what it was to be filled. He stood perfectly still, his hardness pulsing inside my tightness, his body pressed against mine.

'I don't want to hurt you,' he said. Then he kissed me again, sucking my tongue deep into his mouth, one hand under the cheek of my bum, forcing my hips up against his, and the tension in my body rose higher and higher till it burst in a spasm of pleasure so intense that for a moment there was nothing else in the universe. As I came down from the clouds I felt him pull himself out of me, then crush himself against my belly, rubbing himself in the sticky wetness he spurted there, with a grunt. Then we were done.

His body was still against mine for a moment, then he kissed me on the forehead one last time. He didn't meet my eyes as he hitched his clothes up and tucked away his privates. For some reason, he looked kind of defeated, and I pulled the edges of the gown around me, covering my new body, every part he'd touched, every slippery spot sensitive now to the feel of the fabric over it. He paused on his way out of the door as if he had something to say, but then said nothing. His going left me changed.

I was a woman now and I understood everything. Sam and the garages. This was what happened in the darkness, why everyone kept returning. My mother and Berris. This was why they went to bed early. This was what he was doing with her. Not having this was what she meant by being alone. I understood.

I went to the bathroom and this time I showered. My body felt different to me. I felt different. I stood in front of the mirror afterwards examining my face, trying to see if I could see a physical change, wondering whether others might be able to see it even though I couldn't. After I put on my pyjamas, I went downstairs to get my dinner. He'd taken it out of the fridge and left it on the table for me.

I thought about carrying it into the front room, where music played still, where he was, but I couldn't. Something stopped me. Like instead of what we'd done making me feel closer to him it made me feel we'd done something wrong, *I'd* done something wrong. Instead I decided to eat at the table in the kitchen on my own, and I did it as quietly as I could.

He came in while I was still there, and I think he felt the same. He smiled, but it was brief, tight, forced. He hummed as he poured himself a drink, as if everything was normal, but he was styling it and I knew it. He moved quickly and was out the room before I'd had a chance to think of a single thing to say to him.

I wondered whether he was, like me, thinking of what we'd done. Did he see me differently now, and if he did was it different good or different bad? And would we do it again? Should I let him? Then I remembered his wife and I felt gutted. All the things that stood in the way of our love struck me at once: he was Berris's friend, he was much older, he was married, I was still, for two months anyway, a schoolchild. He was probably thinking of these things too, not me, not love, just the wrongness.

Though all of these thoughts should have reduced my appetite, I waxed off the food on my plate as if I hadn't eaten for days. Afterwards, I scurried as quietly as I could through the passage, up the stairs to my room, and for the rest of the night I stayed there, lost in my thoughts, marvelling at my life and all the things that just kept coming at me, at what felt like the length and breadth of the world's experiences, all concentrated inside the smallest possible amount of time.

10

I had to get out. To clear my head. I washed my face and threw on some clothes, desperate to escape the place that for so many years had been my cocoon against the world, the safest hiding place until he came. I shouldn't have let him in, allowed him to weigh me down with his stress-filled tales, his protracted exhumation of all things buried deep. I pushed my purse into my jacket pocket, pulled back the hundred tiny braids he'd plaited into a ponytail, wrapped a scarf around my neck and left. I felt like a tightrope walker who'd been carefully balancing for years, suddenly given a hard boot in the back.

It was Sunday, still early, and the streets of Hackney were quiet. In a few hours they would be as busy as any workday rush hour, but at that time of the morning it was almost peaceful. It was typical English early spring. From inside, through the window, the day looked bright, but what I stepped out into was a biting cold. The sun played without warmth or humour against crystallized car windscreens and on every exhalation, my breath smoked.

The only other people on the streets were sedate, the churchgoers, outfitted in their Sunday finest, on their way to pray. I had never gone to church as a child, never had religion. But that morning I envied them. How I wished I had faith, that I believed in a greater, grander plan, that everything was part of some clever design and for a purpose. More than anything I wished I had it in me to pray.

I walked towards Dalston, my pace brisk yet still too slow when what I wanted to do was run. I turned off Dalston Lane, right on to Ridley Road where the great clean-up was underway from yesterday's market; the road filled with the noise of motor-powered vacuum cleaners and the relaxed chatter of shopkeepers leisurely straightening things up. There would be business done today, Sabbath or not. My pace increased.

This was where she had shopped, my mother, rummaging through cardboard boxes of moist compost for the freshest cassava, the least blemished christophine, delicately breaking ginger root with her fine, slim fingers, pressing and testing the ripeness of the choicest green sabaca. The men here paid compliments to the women who bought from them. They flirted and rounded prices down to numbers divisible by ten.

My route took me up to the high street, past the pound shops with their cheap wares piled high and broad in primary-coloured plastic baskets, past Cash Converters and the charity shops, the bookies and the fluorescent off-licences with their neon-lit signs, past the distinguished undertakers with their high-shine wood and stone exhibited through speckless, pristine glass.

She had told Berris and he had told Lemon. Why had I been left out of the loop? How was it that even dead she still had the power to make me feel insignificant?

Inside the supermarket I took a deep breath of air, chilled and void of odour. The tension in my body began to abate. Here, the produce was set out in orderly rows, the fruits and veg and meat sanitized and attractively presented in neat poly-styrene packages. I found the symmetry calming, the parallel aisles and shelving, the neat-stacked rows, the square labels and barcodes, the clean smooth walls.

I took a trolley, not because I intended to buy much, just for the feel of the roll of the wheels as I wandered round. I stocked up on the essentials; a litre-sized bottle of vodka, a bag of ice and four more bottles of wine. Even to my eyes, the contents of my trolley looked like they belonged to some-one with serious alcohol issues, so I had a wander around the store in case there was anything else I needed. In the bread aisle, I put a loaf of brown bread into my trolley before notic-ing the hard dough bread on the shelf below. I knew Lemon would prefer hard dough, so I took the brown bread out and the hard dough in. As soon as I had bagged and paid for everything, I knew I'd bought too much. Or maybe I should have brought the car with me. In any case, like the ongoing story of my life, it was too late for regret.

Outside it was drizzling. Lightly at first, gradually getting heavier the closer I got to home. I walked slowly, feeling oppressed both by the weight of the shopping and the weather, yet still reluctant to get back to where I lived. It felt like my distress was in direct proportion to the distance from home, and the closer I came to it the worse I felt. I so wanted to cry.

But it was impossible to say what I should cry for. For Mavis? For Lemon and Berris and Ben? For murderers who went to jail or those who lived on the outside in jails of their own making? For the brother or sister I could have had, whose loss was no less for the fact that I hadn't, till today, even known they'd existed?

By the time I took the corner into the road I lived on I was drenched. On the doorstep I put down a bag, searching my pockets for the key. Unexpectedly, the front door opened and Lemon was there, standing inside, awaiting my soggy entry with red-rimmed eyes so shiny it was evident he had been crying himself.

I passed him without a word, through the door, the hall-way, into the kitchen, where at last I was able to put the carrier bags down. He followed close behind me, then as I turned, he half stepped, half fell towards me, hands going up and around my back, crushing me hard against him. He buried his face in the bowl of my collar bone, heaving and snorting, adding his wet distress to the rain on my neck. My body was stiff as he clasped me tight. And over and over and over again, he just kept repeating, 'I'm sorry.'

I laid in the bath for hours, topping up the cooling water regularly, unpicking the plaits he had been so patient putting in. I finished when the hot water ran out. I stood then and stepped out. I was slow to dry my skin and, for the first time ever, I could not be bothered to wash the bathtub out afterwards, so I left it.

He was sitting there, obediently, on the floor outside the bathroom door, like a faithful hound; had maybe been there the whole time I was in the bath, just waiting. I didn't look at him as I walked past and he didn't speak, but I heard the rustle of his clothing as he began to move, following behind me as I entered my room.

He sat on the bed as I towel-dried my hair, discarded the towel, creamed my skin, combed through and then blow-dried my hair. He watched in silence, with an expression I was unable to fathom, but which was not anger or madness or lust.

I felt removed. As though my spirit had vacated my body and broken free to glide overhead, observing my life from a detached perspective, seeing my bedroom, the bed, a weeping man's arms wrapped tightly round himself, a naked woman on a stool, two fingers deep inside a hair-grease tub.

And when I had finished, there was nothing left, not even the energy to find a nightie or a pair of knickers, I just crawled into the bed and he covered me and sat down beside me, gently rubbing the back I had turned on him as I closed my eyes and willed sleep to take me, willed eternal sleep to take me, please. I slept.

He was gone when I awoke naked beneath the quilt. The room was fresh and I pulled the bedding closer around my neck, trying to make sense of what was happening to me. I couldn't recall ever sleeping in my birthday suit. In fact it was so out of character for me that the more I thought about it, the more certain I was that I was having a nervous break- down, and the possibility didn't surprise me in the least. What did surprise me was that it had taken so long to occur.

My son.

I slipped out of bed and went over to the dressing table, into the least used bottom drawer, where I took out a box and carried it back to the bed. I leapt into the warmth beneath the quilt, took my nightie from under the pillow and pulled it on. I opened the lid of the box and there he was, Ben, two months ago, at Christmas, in a photo taken by his dad at his house, in front of the tree, surrounded by presents, eyes round with wonder. Red had invited me to join them but I hadn't. I told him I had already been invited to a friend's, then spent the loneliest day of the year on my own.

His eyes.

Looking into his eyes had always disturbed me. I dug deep down into the box and found a picture of him when he was six months, and there they were again.

Her eyes.

His skin was a shade darker than hers had been, his hair a short crop of shiny jet curls, cheeks fat as hamsters', but there they were, my mother's eyes, love-me eyes, so big you could get lost just staring into them. Was that what kept making it so hard for me to love him? Her?

I went back to the Christmas photo and touched his face. Though not as fair as her he was still way lighter than I was. I had never been able to judge whether he was a good- looking kid or just light-skinned, like some people thought all blonde women were beautiful when in fact they were just blonde. I would stare at him, trying to judge as a parent with some objectivity, not wanting to be one of those people who treated lightness and blondness as some kind of independent beauty criteria. There was no doubt his eyes were compelling, but did they alone make him handsome? I still couldn't say. Looking at him, all I could say for sure was that in that photo he looked happy, utterly happy. And complete.

Was this how my brother would have looked?

Would I have found it easier to love my brother than my son? Or a sister? *Their* daughter. How was it possible to experience grief for someone I couldn't even be certain it would have been possible to love?

And Ben; what was I really doing with him? I hadn't rung him or his dad, hadn't felt outrage or loss or grief at the thought I might never see him again. Instead I was making plans to go to Citizen's Advice. For what? It wasn't as if I actually *wanted* him, wasn't as if I longed to have him here with me full time. If it were that simple I could have gone to the police, accompanied them to Red's and collected Ben, as per my legal rights. But I didn't want that. What I wanted was what I'd had before, nothing more and nothing less: for Red to look after him and for me to have him every second weekend, here, not there, like some paedophile having supervised contact, Red breathing his advice down my neck while taking notes, judging. Because I had given birth to him and I had the right. What kind of reason was that for me to base a relationship on? With as much emotion as you'd find on a yellow legal pad. My feelings had nothing to do with love and everything to do with ownership. What kind of person was I?

I put the photos back inside the box. When I replaced the cover it fell into place as securely as a coffin lid. I pushed the box under the bed and lay back down. The tears came fast and unstoppable then. On a roll.

He'd cooked oxtail and butter beans for dinner, with small round dumplings the size of marbles, brought it to me in my bedroom on a tray, waited while I adjusted the pillows behind my back and smoothed a level space on the duvet for him to put it down. He sat on the bed near my feet and watched as I ate. The meat was so tender it fell from the bone, melting inside my mouth, the gravy spicy and so compelling I found myself unable to stop eating even when the plate was empty, sucking out every crevice of the bones, using my mouth like a bottom-feeder, my tongue like a young girl French-kissing an orange.

I thought I had been creative about food in the past, ensuring a balance of texture and colour and nutrients, attractive to the eye, contrasting on the palate, on inspection, perfect in every respect. But everything he had cooked since his arrival had been divine. I could not recall any dish I had ever prepared that had an impact like this, that was such a dizzying, seductive, overwhelming experience that the more I ate, the more I wanted. Even how I was feeling, with all the emotions I was carrying inside – the confusion, the distress, the impact of new hurt piled on top of the old – my appetite was so great it surprised me.

Like gorging at a funeral.

He watched.

'You want more?'

I shook my head.

'Then we should talk.'

'No more talking. Please. I can't take any more.'

'What no kill you, make you strong.'

'I think it will kill me.'

'You's so like you mum. There's nothing you can't cope with.'

'She didn't cope. She's dead.'

'I can't understand why she never tell you.'

'It doesn't matter.'

'How can anything upset you that much not matter?'

'I don't wanna do this. It's too late. There's no point raking up ancient history. What difference can it make?'

'I have to say it make a big difference to me.'

'Because you *loved* her?' The words were sneered. He *had* loved her, loved her in one of the many forms his love took, love that he chose not to distinguish from envy, or anger, or madness. 'You both did, didn't you? Loved her to death!'

He flinched.

'You's just like him,' he said. 'How he was them times...'

'Don't compare me to him!'

'Cept he use his foot and his fist where you use you mouth.'

'I am nothing like that man!'

'Talking down, talking hard, using love like some kinda dirty word...'

'He was a monster! I am not a monster.'

'Like something nasty stuck to you shoe...'

'You take it back!'

'Like you never loved her too.'

It was my turn to be dumbfounded. Then I laughed. Aloud. In disbelief that anyone could be so stupid. But it wasn't funny and almost immediately I stopped.

'Lemon, you've been good company. Thanks very much for the food. You've outstayed your welcome. I want you to go.'

'You gonna sit here in front of me and say you never loved you mother?'

'I need you to go *now*!'

'Say it. Say, "I never loved her." Then I'll go.'

'I told you I didn't want to do this...'

As I sprung up from the bed, the tray on my lap and its contents spilled to the floor. He didn't glance at them, just reached out and grabbed my arms preventing me from moving any further away. It was the first time since his arrival that I had felt his strength. His hands closed tightly around my wrists and, though I struggled to free them, I was held fast.

'Go on. Say it. You don't have no problem opening you mouth to broke a person down, so open it now and tell me you never loved her.'

As I struggled harder, his hands tightened around my wrists.

'Let me go!'

'Say it first!'

'Fucking let me go!'

'Say it!'

I screamed the words: 'I hated her!' He let me go. 'I hated her! I hated her! I hated her!' I sank to my knees on the carpeted floor in front of him, the strength in my legs vaporized, the rage spilled, exhausted. I didn't look at him. I knew what I would see. Contempt. He wouldn't understand. No one could. It was impossible for anyone to understand the impossible.

'Why?' he asked. 'What you mum ever do to you?'

'Nothing. She did nothing.' When she should have said *Stop*, she was silent. When she should have fought, she ran. I felt his hands, slipping under my armpits, pulling me up, into his arms, enfolding me into his body. He laid his head on the top of mine. I repeated, 'She did nothing.'

'She loved you,' he said.

'She loved him more.'

'Differently!'

'*Instead*. Even Berris knew. It was him who told me.'

'He was wrong.'

'For telling the truth?'

'He said it from spite. Spite is a wicked thing. I don't just say so because I think it, I know because I been there. I sunk to the depths where you do a certain thing you know is well out of order, but you tell youself at the time you was within you rights to do it, how it was exactly what the other person deserve.

'S'where my head was the night he told me 'bout the baby. All I was doing was rocking and listening to me music. For years after, I told myself I wouldn't of said nothing if he did only stop there, that it was his fault, his fault for laughing and going too far. But it wasn't true. I shouldda kept me mouth shut but I let spite open it.'

Suddenly, I felt sick. I pulled away from him and stood up. 'What did you say to him?'

'I went too far.'

I put my hands on either side of my head, squeezing them tight, locking the train of thought inside it. 'You told him!'

I almost thought he had not heard me but then he looked up and I saw in his eyes that I was right. He wore a child's expression: *No matter how badly you think of me, it's nothing compared to how badly I think of myself.* 'Oh my God, it's true. You really did.'

'I never told him everything...'

'What did you say?'

'That you came on to me. That you asked for it...'

'Did you tell him what you did?'

'I told him I said *no*.'

Then I did laugh. Now that really *was* funny. Genuinely funny. I laughed my bloody head off and he watched me in silence till I had calmed down enough to say, 'So you came out of it stinking of roses. That was good. You were good.'

'That was the second time I went too far.'

'So let me just get this straight: you went too far the night of the engagement party, and too far when you slept with me...'

'No! I *shoulda* said no but my head was so full already, there wasn't a drop of space left to think. Any full-blooded man woulda had a hard time saying no to what you was offering on a plate, and having you was like getting back at Berris and having some of you mum at the same time. Then afterwards, separate, was the rest of the feelings that might've come first and natural to any other man in the same spot. What I said to Berris after was where I went too far. Not before.'

I closed my eyes. There was nothing sacred, nothing decent, nothing pure and good and innocent left. Not even the giving of my virginity to the man I loved. He had taken what I had offered and while he did, he'd been thinking of her.

'And the third thing? What was that?'

'Her last night. That was the third and the last time I went too far.' He was quiet for a moment. 'Told myself for years all was Berris' fault; everything I did was 'cos of him, the way he stay, but it wasn't true, I accept that now. When I say spite is a wicked thing, believe me, I know what I'm talking 'bout.'

The words came out of my throat sounding crushed. 'I thought he saw something in me. That I was marked. That somehow, somewhere, there was a sign on me that other people could see. Do you know what he did? What *you* did? With those words?'

Now his eyes were filled again and I was glad. I felt my anger returning and it was like having back a misplaced comfort blanket. I had long ago vowed never again to be wrong-footed by the cruellest of all hoaxes – grown men's tears.

'He hurt me.'

He was ashamed but he did not look away. 'I'm sorry,' he said.

And I could see he was, could see it with my own eyes, but what difference did it make? He had said what he'd said and Berris had changed me, changed me into a person I could no longer recognize, except in my similarity to him.

11

She was in the living room when I entered, sitting on the settee next to Berris, eyes downcast hard. That was the first sign that should have alerted me to the fact that things were not normal, but I missed it completely.

For the whole day my head had been filled with Sam and Lemon. In my mind I'd travelled with Sam: into the car with her and her cases, tagged along on the airport run, watched as she checked in her luggage for good, as she boarded the plane and carefully belted herself into the seat that would take her away and out of my life for ever. And in the moments I hadn't been thinking of her, I was thinking of him, what we'd done, and what the difference was between being a lover and being in love, whether those two things were as jumbled in his head as they were in mine, whether he was thinking of me, and if so, *what* he was thinking.

It had been impossible to concentrate at school, and after lunch I hadn't bothered going back. I went to the library again. Somehow, being surrounded by books made me feel more secure, like there were a thousand stories with a thousand alternative endings, any one of which might be the truth. There I'd spread my textbooks on the table in front of me, trying to make it look like I was justified in being there, giving the impression I was someone with their head cleared enough to be able to study, to focus on the future, though there was so much going on inside my head it was a wonder I could think at all. After, I left and walked around Pembury Estate, then round and over Hackney Downs, and even over to Nightingale, as if everything might have been some huge mistake and I'd see her there, chucking down her bag, laughing and flirting like she owned the place, hooking on to my arm as naturally as if it were some part of her own self, glancing at a single thing, then me, and both of us cracking up without a word being said, because we two shared the same mind.

Emotionally, I was everywhere but in the present. Even so, I still clocked it as weird when I said, 'Sorry I'm late,' and she didn't answer.

'Sorry, is it?' Berris asked.

He was looking at me, genuinely looking, meeting my eyes and holding the contact. As usual, he looked like he knew something no one else did, and kind of smug, like he did when he'd hurt my mum and was challenging me to say something. But there was something else there as well that was out of place and unnerved me, an expression I couldn't put my finger on then and there. Even before I had a chance to try to work it out he spoke again and the steadiness of his gaze and the tone of his voice chilled me through from the outside in.

'Where you coming from this time of night?'

My fear was like an enormous stress. I'd seen his work, what he was capable of doing to her, and I was smaller than my mum. How much easier would it be for him to do that to me? But below the fear, constant and expanding inside my chest, was anger. Just who did he think he was? He was already living free of charge in my father's house, pounding my mum and treating her like dirt. If she wanted to accept that it was up to her, but he had no right to ask me anything or to expect me to explain myself to him. He wasn't my father. If anyone should be asking me anything it was her – and she wasn't. She wouldn't even look at me.

I said nothing and, because I knew the anger would be blazing in my eyes, I looked down at the floor. He walked over to where I stood and stopped in front of me, too close. His feet were planted wide apart. He was wearing maroon leather brogues, with cream socks to match his jumper. Though I couldn't see the sides of them, I knew those ones had large maroon diamonds up the sides. His shoes were immaculately polished.

'You hear me ask you a question?'

I nodded. His shoes moved a fraction closer and I stepped back.

'School done three hours ago. You out looking for man?'

'No!' I said.

He was close enough to slap me and that's what I was expecting. I was tensed hard, expecting to feel the blow any moment, but it didn't come.

'Look at you, with you short skirt...' – his hand skimmed it lightly – '...you blouse open up, everything hanging out.' He flicked my blouse, above my breasts, and I flinched. The top two buttons were undone, nothing big, not like you could see anything unless you came and stood right next to me and looked down it. 'You been out with you man-friend?'

I blushed and shook my head. If he'd said *boyfriend* it might have been okay, but *man-friend* made me think of Lemon. Suddenly it became clear to me and I was terrified. The signs I'd sought in the mirror, signs I'd changed, that I'd become a woman, though I hadn't seen them, Berris could. Maybe not just him but others as well. How could I have expected to change so much on the inside and for there to be no outward sign of any difference? I looked at my own feet and was horrified to discover my toes were pointing outwards. I shifted quickly, turning them in. I wanted to look up to see if he'd noticed, but I didn't dare.

'Liar!' He stretched out the fingers of one hand so they were splayed wide, then examined them. Using the fingers of the other hand he rubbed the skin between his fingers. The rest of his hand looked fine, but the skin there was chapped and in want of creaming. It looked better when he'd finished, but only a little. He rubbed a particularly dry spot one last time. He was like a man out strolling, in no hurry at all. He flexed his fingers then finally spoke. His voice was as gentle as I'd ever heard it. 'Go upstairs to your room.'

*

I began to cry as soon as he walked into my bedroom and closed the door behind him. He held a maroon leather belt in his hands, one that he'd probably picked out especially that morning to match his shoes, and it did. Perfectly. It was doubled over in his right hand, and his left played with its length, running up and down, touching and caressing, as though the feeling it gave him was nice. He said if I told the truth he might not have to use it, but I knew he was lying. I couldn't have put into words how I knew but it was to do with his eyes and the thing I'd seen in them downstairs; the aliveness in them, the thrill, like the look Lemon might have seen in my eyes when he stood still inside me and pressed me against him. If he'd looked into my eyes then, he would've seen what I saw in Berris's eyes as he stood in front of me fingering his belt.

Passion.

No matter what I said, he was going to use it on me and that's why, even before he'd started, the tears had already begun to fall. More than anything, it was the inevitability that really got me.

To *who you been seeing* I answered *no one* and he let fly the first lick. Same question, same answer, the second. The third time he asked, I panicked. I'd never been beaten before in my whole life, ever. Never with a belt. Never felt a crack across my back explode through my body like a lightning bolt of pain. I lunged at him, caught the belt mid-swing like a length of fire against my bare hands and held on, trying to wrestle it from his grip. My mistake was painted across his face in the darkest colours of rage. He fought me for it and won. And that's when the beating really began.

There may be people so brave they would have struggled and done their best to show how tough they were, who would not have given him the satisfaction of hearing them yell at the top of their lungs, who might have been mortified for the whole street to know they were getting a roasting.

I was not one of those people.

I screamed my head off as loud as I could. I called for help, for my mother, for him to stop. I made so much noise, I fully expected to see any moment my mother bursting into the room fighting him off me, that the neighbours would pound the door, then race up the stairs to see what was going on, that someone would call the police and they would kick the doors down and charge up the stairs to arrest the bastard. By the time he'd finally finished with me, out of breath and panting, covered in a light sheen of sweat from his exertions, my throat was as raw as if he'd beaten that part of me as well.

But no one came.

The whole street must have heard.

But no one came.

The whole world must have known what he was doing to me and not a single person did anything to stop him. If I'd thought I felt alone before, it was nothing to how I felt after, lying on my bed, body aflame, full of disbelief and fury, unable to do a single thing about what he'd done to me but cry. Lying there, I vowed I'd never make the mistake ever again of counting on anyone in any circumstance to help me. I'd never expect protection. I had thought Lemon had made me a woman, but I was wrong. I'd been a little girl who'd had sex. It was Berris who'd taken me from the realm of childhood into adulthood, made me like one of those people in the Before and After adverts; the person before the beating, the person I became after. Lying there I promised myself whatever happened in my lifetime, I would always remember I was in it on my own.

And as for my mother, everything I'd ever felt for her, the envy, the confusion, the sympathy, the annoyance, the admiration, the frustration, the love, that man removed every one of those feelings. I had a single feeling left, so thick and complete it would be with me till the day I died, so strong I couldn't even speak it. She'd stood by and let the man she had chosen, the man she brought into my father's house, wear himself out on my skin, without lifting a finger to stop him, not even a word or gasp or whisper. She'd cast me aside and out as if I were nothing. No matter what she said, I would never forgive her, and I promised myself that no matter what came after, I would never forget it.

Ever.

12

In glorious high-definition Technicolor, complete with stereo-surround sound, the memories in my mind played out like the trailer of a film: a baritone roaring, a soprano scream, the ripping of a paper sheet into a hundred tiny pieces of confetti. My mind kept stepping back, trying to keep to the shadows around the edges, resisting, avoiding, terrified, and all the while my heart hammered inside my chest as hard as if it were tunnelling up for air.

I drank.

Enough to have taken me beyond the point of recall, lucidity, or even consciousness. I should have been legless, passed out in an unthinking slump over the toilet bowl, beyond even vomiting. Instead I was awake, alert, drinking more.

And feeling.

He had known she was carrying his child, known that, in killing her, he would also be killing his own flesh and blood, yet that hadn't been enough to stop him. Not just the taking of a single life, but two.

His son.

Their own daughter.

While he was plunging, had the thought even crossed his mind?

Or was it for their baby he had cried? Head back, mouth wide, a primeval creature processing a single emotion: grief. As if he'd just come across her body unexpectedly, and its expiration had nothing to do with him. Tensed veins were raised hard beneath the underside of his skin, corrugating his neck, his arms, his face, and his vocal cords strained to pierce the silence that had followed in the wake of her screams.

Her screams, *those screams*, I still heard them at night. In dreams where I crouched on the floor beside my bed, face squashed into the centre of the pillow, the sides pressed so hard against my ears it made my wrists hurt; in dreams where my eyes were squeezed shut, jaws clenched hard, my lips pulled tight over my teeth; in dreams where I actually prayed for the screams to continue, because the only thing worse than the sound of her screaming was the silence when she stopped.

That night, in my bedroom, the sudden silence had been louder than what had come before, almost static, raising the hairs on the back of my neck, sending a tingling spray of pins and needles over my skin, which took their energy from the strength vacating my knees.

The silence had been like a vacuum. It drowned out the sounds I made as I rose on weakened legs, drowned out my footsteps, the creak of the bedroom door opening, every normal household noise I should have heard as I crossed the landing – the click of the boiler, the whirr of the fridge, the blare of a lorry horn in the distance – drowned everything out. I heard nothing as I opened their bedroom door, not a peep, just felt a shift of air, like a draft brushing upwards, as my legs finally gave and crumpled into a heap beneath me.

There was hardly any mess at all. The room looked so ordinary; everything on the dressing table was in its place, the bed still neatly made. It bore an impression, so innocent, as if someone had sat there earlier to ease their shoes off, or clip their toenails, maybe rested there briefly before drawing the curtains against the night. The normality of the room created a spotlight effect on the bloody splattered couple at its centre, on the floor.

Berris was on his knees beside her, cradling her head in the crook of his left arm tenderly, as if she were a baby, raising her shoulders from the carpet as he pulled her floppy torso against him. The other arm cuddled her around the waist, supporting her back. As if he had forgotten it was there, his fingers were still closed around the handle of 'exhibit one', the knife responsible for blowing away any chance of a lesser manslaughter conviction. The fact that he had taken it from the kitchen drawer, carried it up the stairs and waited for her to come in; 'The very premeditation of his actions,' the prosecution said, 'belie the defence's claim that this was a crime of passion.'

Her floor-length velvet dress bore a harsh rip just above the hem, where she had trodden on it in her haste to flee.

And tripped.

The heel of her right shoe had snapped, and though I didn't notice at the time, the coroner would later note that in the fall she'd bruised both knees.

Those bruises were not the cause of death.

She died from four stabs to the back, deep and clean. He bore not a mark, not a single bruise or cut or scratch, because there hadn't been a struggle. When she should have been fighting for her life, she'd tried instead to run.

He cuddled and cradled her, with his head thrown back, mouth opened wide, emitting a mighty roar that the vacuum swallowed up along with every other sound. Apart from the grotesque horror and absence of music, the whole thing was like a scene from a silent movie.

She let him beat me, and I made him kill her.

Lemon was right. There was no difference between Berris and myself. I had turned into the man I hadn't even wanted to call 'Dad'. I almost laughed at the irony of that cold, steely fact, the truth of it. He had lived with us for around four months, that was all, just over one hundred days out of the thousands I had already lived by then, days I had spent with her, loved her, been fulfilled in her company, even while she had one ear fixed fast on the ticking of the clock. Even now, at thirty years of age, I could no more understand that level of desperation than I had then; the crazy logic that any company, even the company of a man like Berris, was worth dying for, the knowledge that she must have been dying for love for years before he came.

A woman like her.

There were as many different types of love as there were people, Lemon was right about that as well. And my love was like Berris's, to do with ownership and rights, legal-pad-yellow love, camouflaged and cold-blooded and destructive; fine and dandy if you were a single man on the pull for a pretty, rich widow, but I was a mother.

It was, had always been, beyond me.

Throwing back the covers I rose from the bed.

My bladder was full.

I wanted him.

First, I visited the bathroom. Then I went into her room and turned on the light. I opened the cupboard and selected a coat. The floor-length black leather one that flashed a scarlet satin slit. Still inside its dustcover, I placed it gently on the bed. The briefest whisper of settling cellophane, then all was quiet. I went over to her dressing table and sat down on the stool. I pinned my hair back so it was off my face, picked up a powder brush and began.

She had sat here that last night and made herself beautiful. My hatred had been too fresh and consuming for me to watch her, to watch the slow care she took at every stage of the process of transforming herself from merely beautiful to divine. I had seen her when she came back from the hairdresser's, hurrying to be ready in time, rushing to her room, heard her feet going backwards and forwards between here and the bathroom. I'd been downstairs, acting disinterested, feigning an interest in watching the TV, so I hadn't been taken through the transformation detail by detail, in small and tiny steps that made the end result less unbearable. Instead, she appeared before me when her metamorphosis was complete and even I, my head fresh with the memory of skin that stung and welts that wept, with my heart full of rage as piercing and murderous as a blade, even I was stunned.

She was beyond beauty.

Literally, she took my breath away.

She who would soon be dead was dressed to kill. She wore a dress, off the shoulder, in black velvet, with a black satin trim that framed the tops of her arms and fell in waves to sweep the floor, and she held it up, raised it from the hip with a finger and thumb, like some southern belle or an aristocrat, someone totally at ease with fashions that needed assistance to make it through the world intact.

I had seen it then.

Her shine.

I thought it was the contrast of the midnight fabric she was draped in like an exquisitely wrapped treat. I thought it was partly because she knew her body so well, knew how to maximize every essence of the beauty she'd been born with, but that night it wasn't just that, it was more.

She shone.

It seemed her skin shimmered, she truly was glowing, as if for her whole life her beauty had been building up to this moment. The hairdresser had put her hair up at the back and sides, and the top was an explosion of curling gleaming ebony tresses, and a few fell to frame her face, which was fuller, *she* was fuller, with softness and a secret that swelled inside her womb. She had never looked lovelier or more perfect.

But Berris was late.

He should have been home by six at the latest. The party was in south London and they were being picked up by friends who would drop them there and bring them back. They had collected Lemon first, and when he arrived at the house, when he saw her, I know now he must have wanted her to himself for a while, to have her on his arm, to be the one introducing her around, knowing other men were watching with envy, thinking she was his. For such was the nature of his love, drooling and waiting, making do with crumbs, stealing a slightly bigger morsel whenever chance provided an opening.

'You ready?' he asked.

'Berris isn't back yet. I don't understand it. He should've been home long time.'

'Shit. The people them ah wait outside.'

'Invite them in, let them have a drink till he comes.'

'But he need to fresh and dress and everything. I can't ask them to wait for all that.'

'Then what should we do?'

He paused a moment, thinking. 'Come, we go.'

'And leave Berris?'

'Berris is a big man. He can make his own way. He know the people them due here at six. He can cab it and catch us up down there.'

'But he don't have the address.'

'I'll write it down. Jinx, get me piece of paper and a pen.'

A car beeped outside as he wrote.

'Maybe I should stay,' my mother said. 'Wait for him…'

'Don't make no sense me leaving you as you're ready and all,' Lemon said. He tore the sheet off the pad and handed it to me. 'Give this to Berris. Tell him I said we'll see him when he come.'

'Okay,' I said.

'You sure you gonna be okay on your own?' my mother asked.

I couldn't speak to her or meet her eyes. I nodded, looking away.

'I'll make it up to you tomorrow,' she said and she went to kiss me but I turned my face so the kiss missed and flew off into the empty air. She looked at me kind of disappointed, saddened. For a second it was as if she were about to say something, but then she straightened up and the moment passed. 'Don't lose it,' she said as Lemon handed the sheet to me, A4 sized, with hastily scribbled words set out in the centre, like an oversized envelope. The party address.

Don't lose it.

The last words she said before leaving and they expressed nothing but concern for him.

'Make sure you put it somewhere safe,' Lemon said.

'Okay.'

The sky-blue suede coat was draped over her arm. She handed it to Lemon. He smiled as he opened it wide so she could step inside, slip her hands into the arms and ease it on.

He guided my mother out of the door with a hand placed gently in the small of her back, and a moment later, in a mixed aroma of hairspray and aftershave, musky perfume and animal hide, they were gone.

*

I floated down the stairs. I heard music playing, always music: Gladys Knight and the Pips. At the living-room door I paused and peeped though the crack by the hinges, experiencing a frisson of déjà vu.

He made me come and when I did he'd been thinking of her.

He was sleeping, upright on a chair, sitting side on to the table, chin in palm, the elbow supporting his chin on the table, peaceful as a person who had died while dozing. Silently, I stepped inside.

Able to see all of him now, I noticed that his ankles were crossed, one on top of the other, and the top one tapped out the bass line, dancing. He opened his eyes wide. Abruptly the movement stopped. Hastily he stood and looked me up and down. As if it had been handpicked for this precise moment, 'Help Me Make It Through The Night' began to play. He stepped towards me, took me in his arms and smiled.

And it was as it had always been, that this man, this maestro, could always find the magic words through music, the ones that spoke what I needed to hear that moment, or to say, or to have said to me, and there was no more perfect place to be as the track played on than in his arms, his hands inside the coat, playing with the bare skin of my back, my head resting on his shoulder, his own folded over my neck, inhaling the dizzying scent of my mother's perfume as it rose from my body.

We danced.

It was as it had been when I was sixteen, the same headiness, the surprising want I hadn't known I had the capacity to feel. I felt a pounding against my ribcage and I truly could not say whether it came from my heart or his.

We kissed.

It was for me as if it were the first kiss. As if we had risen a few inches from the ground, and the world continued to revolve around our stationary bodies as they hovered lip to lip conjoined.

I felt him.

He moulded me against him, forcing my heat against his hardness, danced that part of his body against mine there.

He danced.

And when the track ended, I began to unrobe him, tugging with desperate hands that shook as I struggled to untie the knot that held his dressing gown together and me outside it. But he put his hands over mine and stopped me. He leaned his cheek against mine and I felt the hot air from his lips fill my ear as he whispered, 'Not here.'

He turned the lights off, asked me to keep the coat on, and we lay down on the bed in the room where my mother had slept and died. The drag of his tongue scorched my skin, and despite the fact that I drenched them, his fingertips burned. In the darkness his mouth found my lips. He kissed them and said a single word, 'Beautiful.' He manoeuvred himself into position above me and when I gasped, I found my lungs filled with her scent. As he repeated the word over and over again, my need grew too desperate for patience, and my release was both swift and intense.

And after, when I thought I was done, gently, he eased me onto all fours on that bed. I felt him shifting himself, shifting me, and in spite of the heat I shivered. Then finally, he took me on my knees like a dog, and I thew back my head and I howled.

13

'Was a friend of a friend's do. A fella from work. Was me who invited Berris and your mother to come. Those days was different, you see, not like now. The chap having it was from Montserrat and them times, any party hold by someone from back home was a open invitation for any Montserratian to pass. You just needed to know where you was going, pick up you bottle on the way, and reach.

'Man, I was like some kinda crazy dog. In some kinda stupid love. Knew full well she was his but I wanted her anyhow. Knew full well she wanted him and I hated him for it. I told Berris the details, but I told him we wasn't gonna leave till eight. Was such a silly lie, because all it took was for you mother and Berris to talk on the subject and they woulda known I give them different information. Was a bit of a gamble, and I already had my excuse to hand in case that happened. Woulda just tell Berris ah no me tell him eight, that I'm sure it's six me say. Woulda say his mind too full up of love for him to think straight. But it never came up. In a way seemed like the gods was on my side. Finally that night it seemed the gods was on my side.

'Man, I felt like Cinderella for true. She spent the night watching out for Berris and I spent the night watching her. I kept thinking this was how it would be if she was mine, if something happened to Berris and it was just me and her. I knew, I knew for a fact, that us leaving without him woulda piss him off something chronic. Knew clear as day that someone was gonna pay for the few hours of pleasure I stole. But I've often wondered since, if I hadda known, truly known how things woulda turn out that night, could I have done different? Would I have waited for him and missed the chance to spend a whole night with her, just we two? And I tell myself of course I'da waited, of course I woulda, over and over, like if I said it the right number of times it would be so, and in my head the answer wouldn't be followed up by the same old question that always mocked me after: *For true?*

'I danced with her and I danced with her and I danced with her. Had Berris've reached, I woulda end up dancing on my own while the two of them cootch up one side holding up the wall, 'cos he couldn't dance but the two steps and she woulda stood up stiff alongside him to keep the peace. But with him gone, man we put down some piece of dancing that night. Wasn't a man alive who wouldna killed to be in my place. Not one.

'How I kept my lips off her, I can't say. All I know is that two o'clock, when our transport was ready to drop us back, I never walked to the car, man, I floated.

'On the way back she started getting worried proper. She knew Berris would be vex. Knew it. She'd had licks for a lot less, and she knew he wouldn't see her going raving without him in any kind of happy light. Me, I played stupid. The man wasn't there on time, so what could we do? We leave him the address, didn't we? I'd had a bit to drink that night anyhow and by that time the dancing was done. I just wanted to get home to my yard, take out on the wife the little excitement that I couldn't take out on you mum. She wanted me to come in with her, but I told her she was being foolish. He would understand, she would see. At the end of the day, she never done nothing wrong, is it? Then don't act like it! But the truth is, I had my own reasons why I never wanted to go inside and face him.

'I knew I had stirred things up, bare-face lie to the man and all, that what I had done to him that night had nothing to do with friendship. I'd been coveting my spar's woman, that was the bottom line, and what with the drinks I'd already had, I didn't wanna fuck up any explanations. Knew he woulda give her a couple of licks, but I thought that woulda been that, afterwards, everything cool as usual, and the three of us just move on. This was what was on my mind as I ease her out of the car and pat her on the shoulder, like *there there, off you go*, then got back in the car and let my man drive me home to my yard.

'Other funny thing that strikes me: I ask my man to wait till you mother got herself inside the house, watch as she root down her handbag for the keys, till she open up the door, turn on the passage light, and give us a wave before she close it back then lock up behind her.

'In my mind, you see, it wasn't safe for a woman to be on her own on the street, late at night. Anything coulda happen to her. You take a woman out, you see her back safely inside her yard, that's the way I was brought up, that's what I was thinking.

'Knowing what I know now, I realize I knew about Jack shit. She woulda been safer on the street. She mighta been alive today if she'd slept the night over Hackney Downs, or in some alley, or on the floor of a shebeen. I waved back to her from where I sat in the car, *grinning*, my mind like a camera, taking her image for ever to visit again and again in the time thereafter; this was how she looked after I drop her home, smiling and waving *at me*. I never hadda inkling, no idea at all, that inside this house was the most dangerous place she coulda ever have step that night. Not a clue.'

He was quiet in the darkness, holding me spooned tightly against him, the leather of the coat between our skins, part of us, rubbing my bare stomach gently with the soft, warm palm of his hand. When he continued speaking, his voice was filled with the utmost weariness.

'And sometimes, over the last fourteen years, some nights I can't sleep and she's on my mind, and I'm wide awake tossing and turning, because the one thing I've always said was that I *knew* Berris. Knew him well, knew exactly how he thought and what he might do. And I find myself troubled, because I think that maybe, when I was wiggling my fingers in the air, and feeling the rock between my legs on the journey home, maybe I knew exactly what woulda happen the moment he got hold of her and there was no one around to help. Maybe I knew.'

He blamed himself. All these years he had been thinking he was responsible. He thought it had all been down to him and what he had done. I knew how that felt, the dark places that kind of thinking took a person. It confirmed for me again that he had never come close to guessing, he had no idea of the part I had played, the responsibility I alone bore. He blamed himself, this man I thought I could love, and it was precisely that reason I was able to tell him the truth, to speak it for the first time since she had died, to say the words aloud that I had swallowed and held down, then spent over a decade pretending they hadn't existed at all. The darkness helped too, the fact that he couldn't see me and I wouldn't have to see his face turn over in disgust. He felt the sudden tension in my body and when his hand stopped moving, it was like a question.

I said, 'I'm the one to blame. It was my fault.'

He actually laughed. 'You was a child. Nothing that happen that night was down to you.'

His mind would not allow him to go there, yet I needed it to. Needed someone else to share my terrible secret, to understand me, needed him to know, this man who'd always known me better than anyone else, who had, like me, made a banquet of jealousy and grudge. I needed him to know exactly who I was and what I was capable of. And I said it.

'I never gave Berris the address.'

*

From the time they shut the front door behind them, my mind was made up and closed to any other alternative. I didn't want Berris around me or in our home or in her life. I wanted him gone and I was prepared to do what I had to do to make that happen.

What right did she have to be happy, to have so much? How did she earn the right to glow like that? What about me and what had happened to me? What about that man and what he'd done? Maybe he had a right to do what he did to her because she *chose* to tolerate and accept it. But he had no right to do what he had done to me, with her knowledge, in my father's house. In my mind, they had both gone too far.

The address.

I looked at the sheet of paper without reading. I had neither interest nor curiosity in the details. It was enough for me to know it existed, his passport to join her on her merry night. Slowly, I ripped it neatly and longways in half, then quarters, then eighths, then into the smallest pieces I could manage. *That* was the act that made the whole thing irrevocable. From then, we were all committed to playing out the scenario I had set up for us, as compromising as a tram track. I would pretend I had lost it, that was the initial plan, or what I told myself at any rate. When Berris came home, I would tell him I'd lost the note and couldn't find it. And that would be that.

I knew him, knew him as well then as I thought anyone could, knew he was crazy. He would drive himself into a rage by the time she came back and when he saw how she looked he would be even angrier. He would imagine men had glanced at her, that they had wooed her, that she had danced with them, rubbed up against them. He might even think she'd thought of leaving him. Such was the train of his thoughts, the landscape of his imaginings. Even though I was only sixteen, the way his mind worked was so elementary a child could work it out.

And I did.

He'd give her the hiding to beat all hidings. Hopefully it would knock a bit of sense into her and she would finally chuck him out and we – as in us, her and me – could move forwards with our lives and Berris would be nothing more than a bad dream we reflected on from time to time. That was what I thought. Or what I told myself I thought.

Then I had to decide what to do with all the pieces. I didn't want to leave the remnants in the bin in case he found them, so I ended up flushing them down the toilet. It must've taken ten flushes to get rid of it all and I still had to pick three floating bits out and roll them into papier mâché pips that I flicked to the bottom of the bathroom bin. After that there was nothing more to be done so I went to my room to do some chemistry revision while I waited. I was calmer than I'd been in weeks and the revision went well.

He arrived back about an hour after they had left, slamming the front door hard as he came in. I felt the reverberations upstairs and that moment was the first time I questioned the unchangeable course I'd embarked on.

Even though he'd just come through the door and had no idea what awaited him, he was already pissed off. I knew the space between him being pissed off and in a rage was gossamer thin.

It was already a thousand times worse than I'd anticipated and nothing had even happened yet. I wished I hadn't torn that piece of paper up and, what's more, flushed the pieces away for ever, but it was too late. I hadn't even read it, so it wasn't as if I could knock out a few of the details myself. At that point my mother hadn't crossed my mind at all. He had come in and I felt afraid, but not for her. Every fearful thought I had, I had for me alone.

He called her. Shouted her name at the top of his voice. If it had been written down, there would have been no question mark to follow the word. He wasn't making an enquiry, it was a demand. Twice more he shouted into the silence. His footsteps pounded up the stairs heavy and quick. I heard the sound of her bedroom door being thrown open and then he swore.

He walked back along the landing to my room and, without knocking, walked straight in and marched up to me so fiercely I thought he was going to grab me or knock me down, but he didn't. He looked like he wanted to though, like it was an effort not to give in to the urge. He paused between each word.

'Where. Is. Your. Mother?'

If there had been a moment when I wanted to come clean it was then, and if I hadn't torn the note up I would have. But with the note gone for ever, it was impossible. If I mentioned it, I'd be expected to produce it, and there was no explanation I could come up with to explain why it had been torn up and flushed away, no explanation that spread the responsibility for that act to include anyone else along with me.

And while all this was going round and round inside my head, the way he was poised, as if any moment he would let loose a cuff or slap or punch, made me feel pressured to respond quickly, to say something, *anything*, and my mouth moved of its own accord and the words simply tumbled out.

'I don't know.'

'*You don't know?*'

'I don't know.'

'What, she never tell you where she was going?'

I shook my head, everything compounding, getting worse the more I spoke, and desperately, I tried to find a way back, but I was already hemmed in by the solid wall that had sprung up behind me, its foundations in my footprints.

'But she was dress up?'

'Yes,' I said. 'She went out with Lemon.'

'Dress up in her fine clothes and covered in perfume, she gone out with Lemon and she never leave word where them a go?'

If only he had stepped back beyond arm's reach, given me just enough space to draw from the air the courage I needed to confess, but he didn't. His voice was in the realm beyond calm, like when he came to my room before to beat me. Like when he spoke after turning the music off at the party. I didn't think about what would happen later, when she did get back and told him she'd given me the address to give to him, had no idea what I would say to him then – if he gave me the chance to speak. Sitting on my bed looking up at him, I knew only that there was no one in the house but us two and that he would hurt me bad. I looked down at the bed as

I shook my head. I sensed him move and flinched, bracing myself for a blow that never came. Instead, he stormed out of the room, slamming the door behind him so hard that it rebounded open with a crash, and with my heart somersaulting inside my chest, I realized I'd been holding my breath and began again to breathe.

He cleaned the house. I could hear him from my bedroom, scraping the bath and the shower out, the wet cloth slapping against the tiles and floor, using so much bleach and disinfectant that even with my door closed, the smell was gagging.

Then he was downstairs, in the kitchen, doing something similar; in the living room, covering every surface with furniture polish and wiping; sweeping the stairs, cleaning down the banisters, then the Hoover was out and he went at it hard, upstairs and down. I'd never even seen him take his own plate to the sink before. I wondered if cleaning was some kind of therapy, a thing you did to contain your anger. It struck me as very weird. But then *he* struck me as very weird. In that respect alone, what he was doing made some kind of sense.

The only room he didn't clean that night was mine and maybe that was because I was in it. Maybe if he had tried to clean my room he wouldn't have been able to keep his hands off me. Maybe he was concerned that, as before, he would have ended up tiring himself out on me, and was making a conscientious effort to preserve his strength for when she finally came back.

I couldn't revise or read or sleep. My head was so full, the only thing I could do was think. I had no idea how I was going to get through the night in one piece, what exactly

I was going to say when she told him, as she certainly would without a shadow of a doubt, that the address had been left with me, in my hands, with clear instructions to pass it to him. Not only hadn't I done that, I'd lied and said I didn't know where they were.

What had possessed me? Why had I done it? The short time I had spent living with Berris had taught me much about fear, how infinite its heights were. Even so, the level I experienced was beyond anything even I could have imagined. Maybe that was why, as the hours slowly passed, it did not even cross my mind what he would do to her, how what I'd said might impact on her. I knew too well how efficiently he could hurt me, and the beating I'd had before had been because he had a suspicion about me, nothing concrete, not a fact. How much worse would my punishment be for this, this lie so terrible it had driven him to clean the whole house?

I heard him making food in the kitchen. Opening cupboards, clacking plates, putting a pot on the cooker, opening and closing the fridge door. My mother had cooked saltfish and ackee before she'd gone out. He gave out coats to say *sorry* and she made food. I could smell it warming up, and when it was ready he called me. Despite the fact that it was late and I'd had no dinner, I had no appetite. I had even less desire to eat with him. But I thought if I didn't go down it would make things worse, which was ridiculous really, because things were already as bad as it was possible for them to be.

In the kitchen, he'd set up two places at opposite ends of the table, the hot food steaming on both. I sat down in front of the plate that had the smallest portions and waited for him to sit down as well. She'd also baked Johnnycakes, and he'd given me two. He brought a bowl of cucumber salad to the table and put it down in the middle of us both. He didn't look me in the face. I thought it was because he was embarrassed.

He'd been crying. Like the day he'd come back with Lemon. His eyes were red, the bags beneath them swollen. His nose was red and he looked as though he was exerting a superhuman effort not to break down and carry on bawling his head off in front of me. I tried not to look at him. I tried not to feel sorry for him. It was beyond me to understand how it was possible to feel sorry for a person who had done what he'd done to me, what he would do to me again once he found out what a barefaced liar I was. My feelings confused and disturbed me. I tried my hardest to focus on dinner, concentrated hard on not glancing his way at all.

He sniffed. Over and over. Like a child. Worse than any child. And picked at the food with such reluctance that a person coming in might have thought *I'd* called *him* down to dinner and told him he had to sit there till he'd finished it. My nerves were stretched to their limit. My mind raced, trying to find a way to work with his distress to my benefit. Surely, if I supported him through this difficult time, it would be harder for him to rip me up afterwards, even when the truth did come out? But what to say? I didn't want to mention the tears. To be honest, he looked as though he was the tiniest fraction away from breaking down completely. Mentioning my mother might not take the conversation in the kind of direction I needed it to go either. I couldn't think of anything other than what I said in the end.

'I'm sorry.'

He was silent for a moment, then he put down his cutlery and picked up the glass beside his plate. It looked like Coke and ice, but I could smell the rum as he gulped, whether from the glass or him I couldn't say. When he put the drink down he was blinking fast in an attempt to hold back the tears, but it was useless. When the dam broke, he began wiping them quickly away, but it was like shovelling before the snow stopped falling and shortly, he gave up and just left them to run down his face.

'Why has she done this to me?' he asked. 'What is it I don't give this woman and she still treat me so, like a fool, like a bups, like I'm some kind of idiot, fucking bitch.'

It was his tone that chilled me. I could not have vocalized it then, pinned down precisely what freaked me out about it, but it was the monotone he spoke in, the lack of passion, love *or* hate, as though he was beyond feeling, beyond hurt, the fact that he spoke like that while crying. It was the incongruity that got me.

'What kinda woman could just up and leave so? Not even care a shit 'bout nothing she left behind, even her kid.'

Stunned, I realized he was talking about me, about my mother and me, about her not caring, not loving me. My greatest fear confirmed by the man who knew. His nose was running now, his face a sodden, slimy mess. Eyes wild. He stood up and began clearing the table, though technically dinner wasn't finished. I leaned back as he took up my plate and began scraping food on to his.

'I'm gonna bus' her arse for her tonight, you watch! I'm gonna teach her a lesson she won't forget. I'm gonna make sure she never does this to anyone again. Ever. And that's not a threat, it's a promise.'

He took the dishes over to the sink, placed them on the side, then turned and left the room.

For the first time, it struck me that bad as my position was, my mother's was even worse. This crazy, violent man would hurt her even more than he would hurt me. And it would be my fault. Not only had I done wrong but, to top it off, I'd lied. I felt guilty and ashamed and afraid. Guilty that my mother would be made to pay for my wrongdoing. Ashamed that I did not have the courage to go to him then and there and confess. But I was in the house with him, alone. Even if I screamed my head off, no one would help me. Isolated and vulnerable, I was afraid.

For myself.

And then I thought about what he'd said and, actually, it was true. She *had* left me behind without a care or thought. That was all she'd done since he'd come to live here. It wasn't just this party tonight, it was her life, their whole lives that I was excluded from. I was the last thing she thought of now.

And my skin still bore the evidence. Too vividly I remembered what he had done, what she had *allowed* him to do to me. When she got in he'd give her the roasting to beat all roastings, a beating so bad that to say sorry, the coat he'd have to buy her would need to be mink, lined with purest silk, and buttons made from rubies and precious gems, and I would watch from the shadows to see whether this time her beaten body would pirouette and curtsy, modelling it before him, all the while smiling.

It came down then like a guillotine, the coldness in my heart, and deliberately I turned my back on any possibility of owning up. Maybe he would beat me, but he would beat me with what little energy he had left after he'd finished with her. Something like glee began to swell inside me then.

Good! Now she'll know how I felt.

On my way out of the kitchen I turned off the lights Berris had left on, then went to my room. I changed into my pyjamas, turned the light off there too, and lay down in the darkness on top of my bed. I felt too awake to fall asleep. So I sat up, hugged my knees and pressed my back against the headboard, listening out for the first sound of my mother arriving home.

'She never stopped him from beating me. Never said a word to me after. Never kissed me or said, "Try and be good, Jinxy", or "My God! He did *that*?" He could've killed me! If he'd had the energy he could've beat me to death and she wouldn't have stopped him. She heard me screaming, she *heard* me and she did nothing. She would have let me die.'

'That's not true!'

'For years after I wondered, what if he'd been trying to kill me? What if it was me he was stabbing? Would she have tried to stop him then?'

'Yes.'

'But she didn't stop him,' I said. 'I loved her and she let him hurt me.'

'Maybe he told her.'

'What?'

'The things I said. About you being…womanish. Maybe she thought you needed it.'

'Needed *that*?'

'A little hard discipline early, stop you turning out loose. Maybe she thought she was protecting you.'

He was trying to make good of an impossible wrong. And if it had been that alone, maybe I could have gone for it like a grateful sucker, accepted his words with a smile, wiped my eyes and moved on with the rest of my life. But it was more. Always more.

'She didn't even try to stop him killing *her*. She didn't struggle or fight, she didn't raise a finger to defend her own life. Even for me. Even if she didn't care that she'd be dead, didn't she care about leaving me alone for ever?'

'She musta been scared outta her mind.'

'She promised me she would always be there for me. She *promised*.'

'She wanted that. You mother loved you.'

'How can you say that?'

'Mothers love their kids. All of them. Even the bad ones.'

'It's my fault she's dead.'

'It's Berris kill her, not you.'

'But if I'd given him the address, he would've gone to the party late. He would've been vex, but she would've been alive. I didn't. That's why he killed her and I think I wanted him to. What kind of a person am I? What kind of person wishes their own mother dead?'

'Even if you had given him the address, it wouldna made no difference. He would still have done it.'

'That's not true!'

'Berris wasn't making it to no party that night. We came and left and he wasn't coming, whether you gave him the address or not.'

'But if I'd given him the note he would've gotten dressed and gone looking for her.'

'Maybe, but he wouldna found her. Not that night. It was always going to come back to him here waiting for her to come in, and when she did, he would have done what he did. Note or not.'

'How do you know that? How can you say that? How can you be so sure?'

'That was my night, our night, me and her. I never meant from the start for him to come. I told him the wrong time. I got here before he did and took her and left. And when he came in, I knew he would be out to track her down, to link up with us and take her from me. So just to be on the safe side, I did the last thing I knew would ensure he never made it, unless he was gonna search the whole of south London that night; I writ down the wrong address.'

'Oh my God.'

'So you see, whatever you did, that night woulda ended the same way. It was her time, and when it's your time, it's your time.'

14

When I awoke, it was dark outside, the day. The early-morning sounds from the street were familiar; closing front and car doors, engines starting, the neighbours setting out as if this Monday was just another ordinary day.

I felt nothing. Lemon had told me what he had told me and I wasn't hurt or angry or relieved or disgusted or amazed or released; I felt nothing. Nonetheless, last night I had vomited, hunched over the toilet bowl. Violently. Alone. Hoping he'd be gone by the time I came out, and when he wasn't, hoping maybe he'd leave during the night. Even though the house was silent, he was still here. I knew it.

As quietly as I could, I left my room and went into the bathroom. Ignoring the dirty bathtub, I brushed my teeth, rinsed my mouth, then splashed my face with icy water. I dried and studied it, my face, in the bathroom mirror, looking for signs, searching my eyes for change, a subtle shift or clue, some physical evidence of what had happened to me; finding none.

Dressed, I went running. In the biting cold. Pausing first to stretch muscles that still ached from Friday, shaking them out before I began, knowing I had taken them to the extreme so recently, wanting to limit further damage if I could. This time I took it slowly. A single circuit of the park, pacing myself like I'd seen other joggers do, but not from any design or plan; it felt natural. It had gone, the drive, the push, the need to flee. I was going through the motions only, feeling nothing. On the second lap of the park, I realized I no longer even felt the cold.

It had been her time.

Had Lemon meant when he said it that it had been my mother's destiny to die at Berris's hands? That it had nothing to do with me or him, that from the moment she'd met Berris and moved him in, she'd purchased a non-transferable ticket to being a murder victim? It went against the little I believed in to accept that. Every person made their own fate. Hadn't I made mine? Lemon his? If my mum had thrown Berris out the first time he'd hit her, she would still have been alive today.

Or would she?

Suddenly I wasn't sure. If she had insisted he went, would he have quietly accepted, packed his bags, wished her a good life and left?

It was on the third lap of the park that something shifted, something inside me.

I felt it.

My feet were no longer pounding the ground, my arms no longer jerking back and forth at my sides, nothing jarred. It was as if my whole body had become an efficient machine, my limbs pistons, and my head cleared so sharply the world and every detail came into focus. I smelled the cold, heard the sounds of schoolchildren's voices and yapping dogs and traffic. Before my eyes the brittle clay landscape fragmented into one thousand different shades of grey and brown. I tasted the salt of my perspiration against my tongue, felt its heat. It seemed at once as if everything was possible and without limits. Like I might gallop or fly. I felt it. And I ran.

My new body showered and dressed, I made my way back down the stairs to where he sat, fully clothed, on the sofa, like a visitor, a neighbour stopping by for a quick cuppa, family passing through. The room was dark and he had turned on no lights. I opened the blinds at the windows. The greenness of the foliage in the garden was intense, wet-vivid.

'Can I get you anything? Coffee?' I asked, and he nodded.

I made it for us both. Four sugars in his, none in mine; poured them into cappuccino cups like bowls, placed them on saucers, and carried them back in. He glanced up at me as I handed him his. His hands shook and the cup rattled against the saucer as he raised it to his mouth and began to sip, even though it was too hot, sucking in air alongside the scalding droplets, making a sound like a percolator.

I waited.

'You decide what you gonna do about the boy?' he asked.

'I don't know,' I answered, honestly. I hadn't a clue. Somehow I had hemmed myself into a tight corner and whittled my choices down to two: Citizen's Advice or letting Ben go.

Become a real mum or forget it. Two options, each with its own unique set of fears. 'I really don't know.'

He looked at me, his yellowed whites red. He had been talking non-stop for three days, taken me with him, up and down and around it all.

That stuff.

Trying to clear things up while there was still time. Working to build up the merits. Did he believe that fate had brought him to where he sat now? That this was meant to be? What about his son, his grandchildren, *his* family? 'And you?' I asked.

'Ain't got no hard plans.'

He started to raise the cup to his mouth again. This time the rattling was even worse. He changed his mind, and put it down on the floor beside the settee.

'What about John?' I asked, and he shrugged. I watched him as he rummaged through his pockets, found the cigarette box, his lighter.

'Did you ask Berris why he said the things he'd said about Mavis?'

'Didn't have to ask. That was one of the reasons he came to see me. He had things to clear up too.'

'And?'

He inhaled deeply. Blew the smoke out slowly. Answered when he was good and ready. 'You know, after what he done, I thought for a long time he was the hardest-hearted man alive, the coldest, the evilest. But after I spoke to him last time, watching him, *listening*, not how I done most of my life but kind of fair-like, not squeezing him into the way

I wanted to think of him, but looking hard to see who he really was, *what* he was, after all that I come to the conclusion he was just sensitive. Oversensitive. Even small things that wasn't meant to be no slight hurt him. I tried to imagine how it felt to be in his shoes, and they was small and tight and uncomfortable...'

'I can't think of him like that. I don't want to,' I said.

'I'm not telling you what to think. Just saying how it was for me. That it was the first time I saw him proper.'

'So what did he say?'

'You know Berris, for a long time nothing, just bawling. Made a hard drink and gave it to him. Made one for meself and the old legs, to keep them straight and strong under me. Watched him cry and thought hard on the way my life had shaped, about Mavis, the things we coulda done, how our lives coulda been. What Berris told me all them years back set us in a direction that was some kinda one-way street; straight ahead only, no u-turns, no reversing; how could ita been anything else?'

'But what did he say?'

'Berris say he couldn't remember a single bad thing I ever done him, how in prison he pass time counting up every good thing, every favour, every *kindness* from me. He said I was the best friend he ever had, the truest, even more than a brother. To be fair was mostly things I'd heard him say before, but always before was kinda said in jest-like, whereas this time, Berris' voice was so solemn, you woulda think is the Lord's Prayer him ah recite. Listening to them thanks made me feel low.'

The coffee had cooled a bit. Carefully, I sipped it and waited.

'All that stuff about Mavis, the things he'd said, none of them was true. "Man, she loved you." That's what he told me. "She loved you. Only you." Maybe *I* need to go prison, to learn to speak the truth. He confessed all to me and I couldn't, couldn't, couldn't do the same. How could I, with me mouth dry like cassava bread? Didn't know where to begin, or end. Couldn't say a word to him about the things I done to him all those years back, not a peep.'

'So he lied? Trashed your marriage on a whim?'

'Seems so.'

'And about ruining decades of your life, what did he say about that? Please tell me he didn't say *sorry*.'

'He asked me to forgive him.'

'Did you?'

'Yes. Can you?'

It was as if the world's axis shifted for an instant, and I felt something like the panic and confusion of missing a step. Berris had taken so much from me. Altered the shape, the potential of my life from everything that had been possible, left me to survive making do with what little was left over afterwards. Forgive him? I could not.

'It's too much. Too soon. Maybe one day I'll be able to forgive him, Lemon, but not today. Not now.'

'I wasn't asking about him. I'm asking you to forgive me.'

And again the tilt.

I wanted to say *yes* to him but I couldn't, because suddenly it felt like forgiving him and forgiving Berris were one and the same. They were both responsible. They had both done it; killed my mum. Only one of the four hands between them had held the knife, but they were both guilty. Either I forgave the two of them, or neither.

'I don't know,' I said and he nodded. He expected no more. 'I want to,' I said, 'but I can't.'

He nodded again.

I took my cup into the kitchen and put it down on the side. There were dirty glasses there and a couple of empty bottles of wine. I ignored them. Three days it had taken, but it was clear now, the reason he had come. I had a strange feeling, a tightness in my chest that was getting harder to contain. I needed to do something, go somewhere, get out. I went upstairs and pulled on some old boots, found my handbag and took out the keys to the car. I couldn't face Lemon again. Not just now.

'I'll be back in a bit!' I shouted as I left.

Inside the car I studied the A–Z, plotting out a route before setting off. On the tail-end of rush hour, it took just over half an hour to get there. Not days or weeks or months. Half an hour to get to a place I had been to the one time and never gone back.

Nothing looked familiar. But then I could hardly remember anything about the funeral. It had been for me as if all memory was concentrated in the fine detail leading up to her death and beyond that there were just snatches here and there for years. I must have been in shock. The thought made me smile. Why should that surprise me? Hadn't I been in shock ever since?

I entered the small building on the right, just inside the gates. Waited till the old guy working there was free and asked him, 'Can you tell me how I'd find a particular grave?'

He pointed to a building opposite. 'Try the office. If you've got the details you can have a look through the register yourself. Or you can pay and they'll do it for you.' He looked at me. 'When'd they die?' he asked.

'Nineteen eighty-three.'

He pointed straight ahead down the road towards a chapel. 'If you wanna take a look yourself just keep going that way. Straight ahead.'

How many people had died in nineteen eighty-three? How many graves would I have to search before I found hers? It seemed easier to return to the office and pay them to tell me where she was, my mother, buried here for fourteen years and I had not visited, even once. But I couldn't do it. I couldn't ask anyone for help. This was a private disgrace.

'Thanks,' I said and, headed in the direction he had pointed, started walking.

There were hardly any people about. The only sounds I heard were birds and the occasional plane. I passed tombs that were ancient. Some said the occupant just 'fell asleep' and I found myself unbearably moved. It sounded such a gentle way to die, having lived first, fully, to simply get into bed one night and not wake up the following day. The way death ought to be. I wondered what had been written on my mum's to explain how she had gone. She hadn't fallen asleep or passed away. She had been wrenched into death. Murdered in hot blood. Did people put things like that on stones?

Beloved mother. Dragged screaming from life.

Past the Chapel of Rest to the end of the road I walked. At the top, I studied the gravestones in front of me. People who died in 1977. Masses of them. To the right there were more flowers in front of the stones than in any other area I had yet passed, the graves being more recent. My mum was buried in 1983. I headed off to the left where the flowers were fewer and the rows of gravestones stretched like incisors into the distance.

I found the graves for the right year but not hers, though I walked the length of the rows slowly, checking every stone. Hers was black. I remembered that. I could tell the plots of those who were truly 'never forgotten' from the ones who had been; the graves visited regularly by the loved ones left behind, flowers brought, notes left. I was searching for the one with the black headstone that looked the most neglected, and that stung.

I turned around when the dates of death went down to 1982. Walked back even slower to the path, then along it. At a junction, there was a triangle of grass with the largest oak tree in it I had ever seen, five or six metres circumference, with a bench beneath it, which I sat on.

It was so quiet.

And peaceful.

That the branches were stripped of leaves made no difference. The tree was majestic. In the summer, was it possible that anywhere in the world there was a more beautiful place to sit and contemplate? Why had it taken so long for me to find it when it had been in that spot for hundreds of years, only thirty minutes away from where I lived? I was bitterly disappointed that I hadn't found her, that I would have to go back to the office and plough through the register like a researcher, felt the disgrace of that weighing on me heavily, that I should need to do something like that in order to find the grave of my family.

My family.

Excited, I stood up.

Directly in front of me were graves from 1967. I walked through a few rows watching the years roll on to 1969. Then I began to walk the rows again. Masses of stones and only the occasional flower here. The too-long dead. Searching and searching and searching. As soon as I stepped into the third row I saw it.

A black heart chiselled from marble. Dulled gold stencilling: *In loving memory of a devoted husband and father, Linville Jackson*; the dates, and below, in brighter golden letters, my mother's name:

who died 1st May 1983
To know her was to love her.

The adjacent grave had a slab of concrete on the ground in front of it. One end had sunk and the earth had risen over it, the grass grown back to cover the earth, and it was as though, in time, even the grave itself would end up buried along with its occupant. But the grave of my dad and my mum was like a garden. The black heart was wrapped in a large red bow. There was a wicker basket in front of it filled with four different plants, the kind of basket you might give someone as a gift. In front of the basket, a band of earth had been cleared and was freshly planted tight with flowering pansies. A sunken vase contained five lily stalks, the buds at different stages of flowering. Two gaped wide in exotic exhibition. The grass before the grave was indented, as if someone had visited regularly and kneeled on that spot. Not Berris. This was the work of years not weeks.

Lemon?

Near the bottom of the stone were two roses beautifully etched into the marble, frosty grey. If they had been coloured they would undoubtedly have been red. She had bought this stone for my father when he died. Had he bought her a space in his plot? It was the perfect place for her. Mr Jackson had always looked after her in life. Loved but not hurt her, cared without breaking her. It was right that he should be the person at her side for the rest of all eternity.

She had promised me she would always be there for me and she hadn't lied or broken that promise. The reason I had not found her before was because I hadn't looked.

I went over it all in my mind, trying to understand the building pressure inside my heart that felt so much like the sadness I had expected to feel when she had died, the absence of which had left an empty space marked out by a perimeter of rage. Inside me I felt a tidal wave building, a tsunami of feeling, as powerful as it was unstoppable.

Fourteen years she had been gone and it had taken me that long to experience grief. My tears when they came were breaking waves crashing downwards, for them, my mum and my dad. For Berris. For Lemon. For Ben. For all that had been done and lost and damaged.

For me.

Then afterwards, kneeling there, I felt like I had ascended into a state of peace, which sat humbled alongside the heartache that had defined every aspect of my life to date. I had wasted so much time, borne so many grudges for so long, and they had made the relationships with the handful of people I had loved in my lifetime impossible. I looked around me at the vast space filled with graves and finished lives and memories. What was the use of grudges when you were sitting here? What was the point?

I would come back. In the week. And bring my own flowers. For them. Walking back to the path I passed another grave like that of my parents', with *Husband* in faded stencilling, and *Wife* added later in newer, sharper letters, and below it, even brighter yet:

And the ashes of their son

And his details.

I was unable to identify the feeling inside me when I read those words, it was too new, a feeling to which I was unaccustomed, but it was so strong I was compelled to stop walking.

I had done everything I could to shun it, employed every measure to help me forget, to pretend it had never existed. Yet in that instant there was no more room for denial. Perfectly still, I let the feeling flood through me, finally recognizing it for what it was.

My mother's name.

Joy.

By the time I arrived back home, there was little left of the short spring day and the house was already in darkness. As soon as I saw it I panicked. I called him even before the front door was properly open but there was no answer. Still I turned on the passage light and the one in the living room. I checked the kitchen then took the stairs two by two. I knocked at the door to my mother's room and at the same time pushed it open and stepped inside.

The bed was made. His things gone. The room as tidy as if he had never slept in it at all. The only sign that he had been here was the window, opened wide, to let the fresh air in.

The ghosts out.

The net curtain rose and shimmied on the slightest of breezes.

I still checked the bathroom, even though, deep down in my heart, I knew.

And I was devastated.

I had no idea where his home was, no number I could call him on, no way of finding or contacting him. When I had the chance and it mattered most, I had not said *I forgive you*, and now that I was ready to, Lemon had gone.

I rang the doorbell once, then waited. The melody went on at length. When he opened the door and saw me standing there he was surprised.

'Hi,' he said.

'Hello, Red.'

He waited a moment for me to say something else and I was unable to decide which of the three million words in my head to say first, so I said nothing. Then he opened the front door wide and let me in.

It was warm, his home. It smelled of burgers and chips.

'I'm sorry, I should have rung...'

'S'no problem,' he said.

The hallway was packed with shoes in two sizes, as if the occupants consisted of a giant and an elf. They were lined up against the wall in ramshackle pairs. There were coats and jackets and scarves strewn over the banister in a heap, and two bicycles were leaned up against the passage wall. I took my coat off and Red took it from my hands, making eye contact, asking questions, seeking answers. I met his gaze.

'Do you want a cup of tea?' he asked.

'Yeah. Sure. Why not?'

'He's in the front room.'

'Okay.'

'I'll get the tea.'

'All right.'

'You want me to come inside with you?'

'Don't be silly.'

'Ben, your mum's here!' he called, then went off and I entered the living room on my own.

He was sitting on the carpet in front of the telly. The room was strewn with his toys. They covered every surface, the settee, the table, the floor. Pictures he had painted and drawn were Blu-Tacked on to the walls. A shelf above the TV housed videos and DVDs; children's ones and family films. There were photos of Ben at every focal point, on top of the TV, above the mantelpiece, and larger ones in heavy frames dominated the window ledge. I thought about his custard-coloured bedroom and felt ashamed.

'Hello, Ben,' I said.

He looked up from the colouring book he was scribbling in, then he looked back down.

'Hello.'

I picked up a muscular male doll in a karate pose from the settee, then sat down in the cleared space, close enough to touch him, though I did not try.

'I'm sorry. I shouldn't have hit you. It was wrong of me. It won't happen again.'

He didn't look up or answer. I was unable to detect even the slightest variation in the rhythm of his colouring-in. I felt the old frustration seeping back and I took a deep breath, trying to check it. I looked around the room wondering how they both managed to live among such chaos and disorder, how they were able to find the space inside it to think. Red came into the room. He looked both pleased and bemused at the same time. Like a person who had come upon the right sign in the right place, unexpectedly. He stared at me as he held out the mug.

'I didn't put in any sugar...'

'That's fine.' It was hot in my hands.

'I wasn't sure if you still took it the same...'

'Yep. Exactly the same.'

'What have you done? You look different.'

'Do I?'

'It suits you.'

'I haven't done anything.'

'Maybe it's love.'

I laughed. Ben looked up. 'Lemon's just a family friend, that's all,' I said.

'Whatever,' Red answered. 'Hey, Ben, you gonna stop that and come and say hello properly?'

'It's okay...' I said quickly.

'Come on,' Red said as if he hadn't heard me.

Ben stopped. He put the crayon in his hand down on top of the page and looked up at me.

Those eyes.

He had her eyes. *My* eyes. I do not know how I had a problem before working out whether he was handsome or not but I had no problem then. The feeling I had inside me was so powerful, I felt weak. I wanted to grab him to my breast and crush him there, kiss every inch of his face, or maybe cry. He was probably the most handsome boy I had ever seen in my life.

So alive.

How had I not seen it before?

He stood up slowly.

'Give your mum a kiss, son.'

As I was putting the mug on the floor beside the settee, politely he leaned over and kissed my cheek, and before he could move back out of reach, I touched him gently, his small head, skiffled low. The short hairs against my skin were springy and soft. The warmth from his head and the heat of my palm became one. I ran my hand over him slowly and the feeling inside me intensified. It was as if he were the first thing of beauty I had ever touched.

Without prompt he moved to sit on my lap and slowly, afraid he would change his mind and get back off, I put my arms around his waist. He smelled of biscuits and ketchup and citrus, and below that something faintly manky, like earth. I wrestled a desire to squeeze.

'How was school today?'

'Okay.'

'You do anything nice?'

'I played with my friends.'

'What did you play?'

'Kites and Globby Heads,' he said.

I scoured my memory banks for some recollection of a game by that name, but came up with nothing.

'How do you play it?' I asked.

'We take off our coats and run around the playground and pretend they're kites. Then we put our coats on top our heads and call each other "Globby Head".'

It was, without doubt, the most pointless pursuit anyone had ever explained to me. My son had spent the best part of his day playing the world's most ridiculous game. I looked into his face to see if he was going to wink at me, or if the corner of his mouth was about to crack a smile, whether his lips were parted in preparation to say the word *Gotcha!*

But his expression was solemn. I could see no humour twitching there. Not only had he just said what he'd said, but he was completely sincere. He really meant it. The welling inside me became impossible to suppress and helplessly, unable to resist a moment longer, I squeezed him tight, then kissed his perplexed face.

And laughed.

Acknowledgements

For their contribution to shaping *A cupboard full of coats*, for every suggestion and criticism, I would like to thank my first readers to whom I am indebted; Elizabeth Galloway, Danielle Acquah, Hilary Facey, Shawn Beckles, Jaclyn Griffiths, and most especially, Olcay Aniker.

I would like to thank Nicky Marcus, who discovered me, and Eve White, my agent for her belief in my novel and her determination.

I would like to thank Juliet Mabey for her enthusiasm and application and the team at Oneworld Publications who could not have been more constructive and supportive throughout. Additionally, I wish to thank Sarah Coward, most thorough of copy-editors, for every astute observation and her help with the fine-tuning.

I consider myself incredibly fortunate to have a need to say to the friends and family who have given me the understanding, support, encouragement, and space to finish this novel – yes, you know who you are! – from the bottom of my heart, I am grateful and I thank you.

And finally, my love and thanks to Colin Edwards, whose stability both liberates and empowers me to write.

Yvvette Edwards grew up in Hackney and con-
tinues to live in East London with her family. *A
Cupboard Full of Coats* is her first novel.